D0388584

What readers are saying about the Daybreak Mysteries:

"*Storm at Daybreak* helped me through a broken romance. . . . I've read the book at least four times and had my faith re-anchored each time."

"I've discovered gold when I came upon your books—indeed a rare treasure!"

"Today I finished your book *Vow of Silence*. I picked it up two days ago and haven't been able to put it down."

"I have read hundreds of Christian novels. . . . I want to tell you that yours surpasses them all."

"As a church librarian, I want to tell you how well received your books are to our people . . . and at many other church libraries."

"We all agree you are tops in fiction, and we anxiously await any new books coming on the market."

What the media is saying about the Daybreak Mysteries:

"Dramatic Christian fiction at its best . . . "
  Christian Retailing

" . . . a fast-moving, spine-chilling story that weaves the Christian message throughout its pages."
  Librarian's World

"Christianity right at the grass roots, in your lives, where you live . . . "
  WCRH FM, Williamsport, Md.

"Hoff is an excellent storyteller who spins a tale that can be enjoyed by men, women, and younger readers alike."
  The Bookshelf

Vow of Silence

B. J. Hoff

Tyndale House Publishers, Inc.
WHEATON, ILLINOIS

Copyright © 1988 by B. J. Hoff. All rights reserved.

Cover illustration copyright © 1996 by Ron Finger. All rights reserved.

Scripture quotations are taken from the *Holy Bible,* New International Version®. NIV®. Copyright © 1973, 1978, 1984 by International Bible Society. Used by permission of Zondervan Publishing House. All rights reserved.

Library of Congress Cataloging-in-Publication Data

Hoff, B. J.
  Vow of silence / B. J. Hoff
    p.   cm. — (Daybreak mysteries ; 4)
  ISBN 0-8423-7195-8 (sc)
  I. Title.   II. Series : Hoff, B. J.   Daybreak mysteries ; 4.
PS3558.03495V6   1997
813′.54—dc20   96-43753

Printed in the United States of America

01 00 99 98 97
7   6   5   4   3   2   1

FOR DANA AND JESSIE

Answered Prayers
And Dreams Fulfilled—
Gifts of Love Forever

A Voice is heard within the quiet spirit,
A Word comes in the silence to impart
The promise of a loving Father's keeping
Of the soul with a surrendered, trusting heart. . . .

B. J. Hoff
From *Gifts to the Giver*

In the dim and drafty room, the man's hands felt chilled as he spread the silky clown suit out on the bed. Meticulously he laid out the baggy white pants, then the oversized tunic—white on the left side, black on the right, topped by a frilly white ruff. He smoothed both pieces, draping them just so, then stepped back to consider the overall effect.

Satisfied, he reached into the open suitcase at the foot of the bed and took out a black skullcap and a pair of white gloves. The gloves he laid on top of the tunic, but the small black cap he examined for a moment, twirling it on the tip of his index finger. At last he placed it just above the white ruffled neck of the tunic and retrieved a red plastic makeup kit from a chair near the door. He aligned the kit neatly on the bed alongside the other items.

The man moved to check the contents of the suitcase one more time. Reassured that the second Pierrot suit, identical to the one laid out on the bed, was still folded in place beneath the few pieces of clothing he had packed, he closed the lid and locked the suitcase.

Once more he appraised the costume and its accessories, finally nodding with silent approval. Then a thought struck him, and he pulled his wallet from the back pocket of his jeans, sliding a photograph out from behind the lining of the bill compartment.

The only light in the room was a weak slice of afternoon gray filtering through a solitary window. He had to hold the photo close, at eye level, in order to see it clearly.

Enormous smoke blue eyes gazed out at him above a smile touched with shyness and a distinct hint of mischief. Silver blonde hair fluffed randomly about an oval face that was part pixie, part angel. It was an incredibly lovely face, wistful yet radiantly alive, unaware of its subtle, haunting beauty.

Moments passed as his gaze searched the eyes in the picture. He flinched when an unexpected gust of wind rattled the narrow windowpane. When he looked back at the photo, a smile spread slowly across his face.

His eyes left the photograph and drifted to the clown suit on the bed. "I hope you're bright enough to appreciate the irony in all this, Whitney-love: the silent clown, about to invade your silent world."

The smile faded, and he pressed his lips into a tight line. It was time. Time to get ready for Whitney. He retrieved the makeup kit from the bed and took it and the picture with him into the next room, where there were two windows and more light. On one end of a rough wooden table sat a swivel makeup mirror, and he scooted his chair in closer, scrutinizing his reflection. Satisfied that he didn't need a shave, he carefully tucked the photo into a corner of the mirror and folded his hands on top of the table.

"So I've finally found you, Whitney," he said conversationally, wringing his smooth, well-manicured hands until his knuckles turned white.

Abruptly, he pulled one hand free and leaned forward to trace the outline of the face in the picture. "I've planned something very special for you, little girl. Not like the others. This is going to be quite a performance. The best yet."

His eyes scanned the room. "Everything's ready for you. Planned, prepared, waiting. Just for you, Whitney-love."

A bundle of rope and a coil of wire lay side by side at the other end of the table. Only inches away were a .38 revolver and a pair of handcuffs. A length of chain was wrapped loosely around the back of the chair across from him.

He leaned a little closer to the photograph. Pressing his finger hard against the surface of the picture, he began to jab at it repeatedly until the mirror toppled, breaking the silence of the room with a clatter.

He pushed away from the table, his chair screeching on the wooden floorboards as he jumped up. The picture had fallen free from the mirror. He yanked it off the table and flung it angrily to the floor.

Unmoving, his breathing quick and ragged, he stared down at the photo. Then, slowly and deliberately, he began to grind it under the heel of his boot, digging at it over and over until it crumbled beneath his foot.

"It's payback time," he whispered. "And you've got a lot of paying to do, little girl. A lot of paying."

ONE

Shepherd Valley, West Virginia
Late October

JENNIFER leaned into Daniel's large, solid warmth, wishing she had heeded his advice to wear a heavy parka instead of her lighter stadium jacket.

The evening was frigid, but Shepherd Valley residents didn't pass up their favorite street festival for anything as insignificant as falling temperatures. They simply bundled up and huddled a little closer together to enjoy the fun.

Spying a small wood-carving booth on the other side of the street, she tugged at her husband's arm. "Wait, Daniel, there's a display over here I want to see."

Daniel gave Sunny, his golden retriever guide dog, a short command, and allowed Jennifer to lead him to the booth across the street.

"Oh, Daniel, I wish you could see this! It's absolutely beautiful." Jennifer admired the country scene in silence for a moment, then clasped her husband's hand and carefully placed it over the center of the carving. "It's a farm. It even has a wire fence and a windmill."

Daniel skimmed his fingertips over the three-dimensional carving. "The barn, right?"

"Yes. Feel right here, above the barn door," Jennifer said, guiding his hand. "It's a hayloft."

"What's this?" He frowned, brushing his fingers from corner to corner over the upper area of the carving.

1

"Snow," she told him. "And it looks so real, you can almost feel it falling on your face! Oh, Daniel, do you think we could buy it for the house? It would be perfect—a barn for our barn!"

Years ago, Daniel had remodeled an Early American barn into a stunning home that had eventually become a community landmark and conversation piece. Even though he had offered to buy a more traditional house for them after their marriage, Jennifer wouldn't hear of it.

"How much?" he asked, his expression skeptical.

Jennifer looked at him. "How much?"

"For the carving."

"Oh—yes. The carving."

One dark brow lifted. "That much, huh?"

"It *is* art, Daniel. Genuine art isn't cheap, you know."

The other brow went up. "Give me a hint."

"You could take it out of my salary."

"You're already in the red, darlin'. How much?"

"My Christmas bonus?"

"A bonus wasn't included in your contract, Jennifer."

"Neither was marriage to the boss."

"That's called a fringe benefit." He stroked one side of his dark beard, flashed a sudden smile in her direction, and said thoughtfully, "I suppose we could work out a deal on the picture, if it means that much to you."

Jennifer sighed. "What kind of a deal?"

"You know that Piney Ridge brunch next month? The awards ceremony for the winners of the state economics essay contest?"

"Oh, no," Jennifer said, crossing her arms over her chest. "No way. Definitely not."

"Honey, you'd enjoy it. They're having bagels and veggies—I know how you love your veggies—and no more than a dozen or so speeches." He paused. "I agreed to have the station cover it."

"Fine. I'll drop you off and pick you up when it's over."

"Oh, *I* can't go, Jennifer. Didn't I tell you? The brunch is the same day as the church's pancake breakfast. Gabe and I are already committed to the meal at the church."

Jennifer rolled her eyes at nobody in particular.

"*Someone* has to go to Piney Ridge. I promised," he said virtuously.

"You know, I don't think I want this picture after all," Jennifer said, watching him. "I believe the barn is a little crooked. And the hay is definitely going to seed."

He shrugged. "Too bad, darlin'. It could have been yours."

"Oh, all *right!* I'll go to the brunch. But there's no one in the booth, Daniel. What if someone else buys the picture before we come back for it?"

"Don't worry, you can still go to the brunch," he said, taking her arm. "A deal's a deal."

She tried to clip him on the ankle, but he hugged her hard against his side, laughing. "Where are we supposed to meet Whitney?"

"At the high school concession stand. I think we're headed in that direction now."

Jennifer scanned the street for a sign of Whitney, but the petite new director of the Friend-to-Friend Association was too small to spot easily in a crowd.

With Sunny guiding Daniel flawlessly along the congested street, they walked on, occasionally slowing down to exchange greetings with friends or browse an exhibit. In spite of the cold, a carnival-like mood prevailed. The festival was not only an annual reminder of the town's heritage, but it also served as a last light-hearted fling before the arrival of another mountain winter.

The entire downtown area had been cordoned off. Hundreds of people poured through the streets, milling about in large and small groups. A mixed chorus of laughter bounced from sidewalk to sidewalk, and a pungent blend of food aromas spiced the air.

Music echoed all around them—folksingers, school bands, and a variety of ethnic ensembles had staked a claim on almost every unoccupied square of ground. Clowns, some with drums, others with balloons and flowers, scampered in and out among the people. Turn-of-the-century, ivy-covered buildings gazed stoically down on arts-and-crafts booths, while dignified stone office structures shared their space with cotton-candy trailers and popcorn stands.

Jennifer glanced up at Daniel and saw that he was enjoying himself immensely. In a warm rush of love for the big, gentle man beside her, she tightened her hand on his forearm. Still smiling, he freed his arm to slip it around her shoulder.

"You haven't seen Jason anywhere, have you?" he asked.

"Not yet. If I know our boy, he's pigging out with Gabe at one of the junk-food stands," Jennifer said dryly. Jason, their nine-year-old son adopted shortly after their marriage, was being treated to an entire evening at the festival by his Aunt Lyss and Uncle Gabe. Jennifer wasn't surprised they hadn't run into him; no doubt he was having the time of his life. "I'm glad he's spending the night with Lyss and Gabe," she told Daniel. "Lyss handles tummyaches much better than I do."

She stopped at the sight of Whitney Sharyn, who was standing a few feet away. "Daniel, this way—Whitney's right over here." She waved, trying to get Whitney's attention, but the small, fair-haired young woman was intent on watching Beulah Wilson whittle oak ribs for one of her custom-woven baskets. Jennifer started to call out, then shook her head as she realized that she had again forgotten about Whitney's deafness.

As they started toward the booth where Whitney was standing, Jennifer wondered about her recurring instinct to look after her new friend. It wasn't Whitney's deafness, she knew. She had sensed from their first meeting that Whitney, like Daniel, had accepted the limitations of her disability and had gone on to make a quality life for herself—a life that was rich and productive, marked by a vital Christian faith and a natural, untiring zest for living.

Unlike Daniel, however, who had been blinded only a few years earlier in an automobile accident, Whitney had lived with her disability from the time she was five years old. A particularly virulent attack of meningitis had robbed her of her hearing.

Being deaf hadn't hindered Whitney's career, however. She continued to amaze Jennifer with her sharp organizational skills, her smooth efficiency in directing the entire program of an assistance organization for the disabled, and her interest in and concern for other people.

Still, Jennifer sometimes sensed a sadness about Whitney Sharyn that puzzled her. When first hired for the directorship, Whitney had revealed little in the way of personal information, only those facts required by the employment application. Even now, three months later, her background remained shrouded in mystery.

Although Daniel often accused her of trying to mother her new friend, Jennifer thought her protective attitude toward Whitney was a response to the vulnerability that seemed to hover about the young deaf woman. Jennifer suspected that Whitney had been badly hurt, either physically or emotionally. She saw subtle but unmistakable signs that Whitney Sharyn had survived some excruciating ordeal. She had survived, but not without scars.

There were little things, Jennifer insisted to Daniel, that simply weren't quite right. Somewhere behind those enormous smoke blue eyes she was sure an old sorrow burned, a grief that continued to simmer. The gentle mannerisms, the winsome smile, and the serene air of assurance were touched with a hint of sadness that never quite disappeared.

Jennifer was convinced that Whitney lived with some secret that refused to give her peace—something that even now caused her great pain. And although she found it impossible to explain, even to Daniel, her instinct wasn't so much to *mother* Whitney as it was to help her find healing.

Whitney's greeting called her back from her reflection.

"I've been . . . looking for you," Whitney said as they approached, accompanying her faltering but precise speech with sign language. Whitney's speech was slow, with an occasional stammer, but clear and remarkably distinct for one who had been deaf since early childhood. A graduate of Gallaudet in Washington, D.C., a liberal arts college for the deaf, she had taught at a Louisville school for the hearing impaired for almost four years before moving to Shepherd Valley. Although an expert lip-reader and fluent verbal speaker, Whitney's experience teaching in sign language had stayed with her, and she often signed as she spoke.

"Where is Jason?" she asked now, smiling.

"He's with Gabe and Lyss," Jennifer said, facing her so that Whitney could read her lips. "He's staying overnight with them after the festival."

"There goes my . . . partner for the rides," Whitney said, pulling an exaggerated pout. After a moment, her face brightened. "Look, Jennifer!" she exclaimed. "The little tramp!"

A diminutive "hobo" was leading a company of other clowns, pulling plastic flowers out of a friend's ears as they approached. The expression of bewildered surprise on his painted face sharpened with each blossom he retrieved. Spying the attentive Whitney, he raced up, bowed dramatically, and presented her with an enormous daisy.

Two of the other clowns also rushed up to her, bumping their comrade out of the way in their eagerness to offer Whitney the contents of their pockets. Laughing, she lifted both hands in protest at their antics, good-naturedly refusing their gifts of tissue carnations and colored bandannas.

"What's going on?" Daniel asked.

Jennifer glanced up at him. "Sorry, darling. Whitney seems to have captured an entire circus of clowns. They're trying to outdo each other for her benefit. Oh, there's one of those—what do you call them—the ones that wear the black-and-white tunics and the little black caps?"

"A Pierrot?" Daniel offered.

"That's it. My dad calls them 'classy clowns.'"

She watched as the Pierrot scampered up to Whitney and began to pantomime in a bid for her attention.

It occurred to Jennifer that the mime was too big for his role and not as graceful as he obviously believed himself to be. *His makeup needs work, too,* she thought. The clown white on his face looked as if it had been applied with a can of spray paint. It leaked into the small tufts of hair that peeped out from under his black skullcap. His wide red mouth was decidedly crooked, and the black paint outlining his eyes was badly smudged.

When the Pierrot's glance flicked from Whitney to Jennifer, she felt an irrational chill. The mime simply wasn't . . . *clownish.* But, then, she'd always been a little peculiar when it came to clowns. For some inexplicable reason, she had always found them more frightening than funny.

Jennifer shook her head at her own foolishness and watched Whitney, who still seemed to be enjoying the clown. The Pierrot performed another brief pantomime, then bowed in a fawning, dramatic manner. Immediately he glided into a fluid, slow-motion routine, which Whitney obviously found enthralling.

Losing interest, Jennifer turned back to Daniel and Sunny. Daniel, apparently attracted to the sound of music nearby, had moved to stand just inside the oval lawn, listening to two young men play a fiddle and a dulcimer.

Jennifer glanced back at Whitney, whose attention was still focused on the clown, then went to join Daniel.

He was smiling and tapping his foot to the beat of the music while Sunny sat contentedly beside him, her head cocked with interest. Jennifer recognized the two musicians, brothers who attended the same church as she and Daniel. The older of the two, flame-haired and fully bearded, was playing a sparkling hammered dulcimer. His darker-haired brother accompanied him on the fiddle.

A vague, burning sensation in her stomach reminded Jennifer that she hadn't eaten since late morning. "I could do with some food, Daniel," she said, taking his arm. "I'm sure I can't make it around the block without an infusion of at least two thousand calories."

"Name your poison, darlin'."

She wrinkled her nose. "Poor choice of words." A concession stand beckoned only a few feet away, and she tugged at his arm. "Come on, Daniel—I smell chili dogs."

"I had a hot dog for lunch," he groaned.

"Whose fault is that? I offered to share my yogurt and peaches."

He grimaced. "Baby food."

"It's good for your skin."

"Most babies are red and wrinkled."

"Only the ones who don't eat their yogurt and peaches." Again she pulled at him. "I think I'll have *two* chili dogs."

Daniel gave Sunny her forward command, and they started off. "Where's Whitney?"

"She's still watching the clowns. The mime was treating her to a private performance," Jennifer explained as they crossed the lawn. "She's right over here."

She pressed Daniel's forearm to slow his pace, at the same time searching for Whitney in the crowd still milling around the clowns.

"Well, she *was* right over here." Jennifer stopped a few feet from the corner where Whitney had been standing only moments before. At least twenty people were clustered near the sidewalk, watching the clowns do a series of acrobatic routines.

Whitney was nowhere in sight, nor was there any sign of the Pierrot.

"That's odd. They were right here."

"They?"

"I told you, Daniel, she was watching one of those clowns." Anxiously, she continued to scan the crowd.

No Whitney.

Jennifer tried to swallow, but her mouth had gone suddenly dry. "Daniel, I can't find her."

"She probably went looking for a snack."

"No, I don't think so," she said. "Whitney doesn't like wandering around in a crowd any more than you do."

"She's probably right around the corner." Daniel paused. "Jennifer, Whitney is a grown woman. You don't have to stand guard over her."

Most likely she *was* overreacting, Jennifer told herself. But she couldn't stop her growing uneasiness. "It's just that she can't hear, Daniel—"

"And I can't see," he countered evenly. "But I don't necessarily need a keeper. And neither," he said pointedly, "does Whitney."

"I suppose you're right," Jennifer said, sighing. But she continued to peer into the crowd, fervently wishing she hadn't left Whitney alone.

Whitney isn't alone, she silently reassured herself. How could anyone be alone when surrounded by hundreds of people in the middle of the street?

"Come on," Daniel said, a good-natured note of resignation in his voice. "We'll walk around and see if we can find her."

Amused with the Pierrot's playful charm, Whitney watched him, laughing as he bowed, strutted, and scampered, stopping every few seconds to make an exaggerated bid for her approval. When it occurred to her that she was actually moving away from the Kaines and the rest of the crowd, she stopped.

Seeing her hesitate, the mime pranced up to her. He lifted a hand to get her attention, then pointed to something overhead, just beyond a couple strolling along the sidewalk in front of them. Abruptly, he darted past the man and woman, motioning for Whitney to follow.

Whitney hesitated. Even though the Pierrots—the silent clowns—had always intrigued her, this one wasn't the best she'd seen. He was amusing—but not *that* amusing. She was also uncomfortably aware that most of the festival crowds were now behind her. There were no booths or exhibits at this end of the street, which actually led to one of the festival exits. Darkness had fallen, and although the lighting was adequate across the street, on this side it was dim—shadowed and distorted by the buildings that hovered over the asphalt. The only people close by were few and scattered.

The Pierrot, however, was still shuffling eagerly from one foot to the other, pointing upward, toward the roof of the Mountain Savings Bank. Instinctively, Whitney went on, but only a few steps farther. Again she stopped, her gaze following the direction in which he was pointing.

A narrow alley dissected the block, bordered on one side by the weathered-stone bank building and on the other by a shoe store. The clown skipped back to her, smiling as he glanced from Whitney to the roof of the bank. Whitney let her head fall back, straining to see what had captured his attention.

Suddenly, the sky spun out of control as she felt herself hauled backward. She had no time to react. Her feet went out from under her, and a white-gloved hand covered her mouth. At the same time, her arm was wrenched hard behind her back.

The clown began to drag her roughly down the deserted alley, away from the lights of the festival . . . away from help. Terror roared through Whitney, overwhelming her, disorienting her. She could *feel* his rage, knew herself to be in the grip of a senseless fury. The mime's hand on her mouth was a vise, mercilessly silencing her.

Her arm felt as if it would rip free of her shoulder at any instant. Nearly wild with fear and dazed with pain, Whitney's mind struggled to blot out the dread reality of what was happening. But memories of another time, of a brutal, crazed violence that had been unleashed upon her, came crashing full force against the present horror, and she felt the first nauseous wave of unconsciousness swell over her.

Fighting desperately to regain control, she tried to stiffen her body, to slow his momentum, the ease with which he was hauling her down the alley. Her peripheral vision saw nothing but darkness until she seemed to be hurtling down a tunnel toward a terrifying unknown. She bit at the gloved hand over her mouth, twisted in his arms, tried to wrench herself free.

She felt him falter, and in that instant she tried to yank her arm loose. The hand over her mouth slipped, and Whitney screamed— not for help now, she was beyond that. Not even for mercy, but for release—release at any price. For she knew what awaited her if she didn't free herself. She *knew*, and the thought was enough to drive her to the precipice of madness.

Enraged, her abductor swung her around to face him with such force that Whitney thought her neck would snap. The grotesque white face scowling furiously at her was no longer the face of a clown, but instead a savage mask of evil. The black paint around the eyes was smeared, the crimson mouth a bloody slash of rage.

Panic seized Whitney by the throat as she stared into the diabolical face. She looked into his eyes and saw the fire of raw fury blazing out at her.

She managed to bleat out one more thin cry before the clown raised his hand, then slammed it against her face.

This can't be happening! Not again! her mind protested.

But in that terrifying instant, she knew it *was* happening again. The darkest of her nightmares had become reality.

TWO

S HE wouldn't have come this way," Jennifer said worriedly. "There's nothing over here but the exit." Holding on to Daniel's arm, she waited for him and Sunny to start across the street.

"We've come this far," Daniel said, stepping off the curb. "Let's go on down the block. If we don't find her, we'll go back to the oval and wait there."

It was darker on this side of the street and nearly deserted, except for the far end of the block, where a few people were passing between the sawhorses that had been set up as blockades.

"You think I'm being foolish, don't you?"

His answer surprised her. "No, I have to admit it's not like Whitney to just wander off without saying anything. Not for this long, anyway."

Something was wrong. Jennifer knew it; she could feel it. She wavered between her growing anxiety and an attempt to convince herself that she was overreacting.

They passed the dark glass storefront of the office-supply center, then Kellerman's Pharmacy. With the amber glow of the streetlight now behind them and only faint scattered shots of light from the festival to break the darkness, the street was deeply shadowed. Jennifer felt a peculiar sense of relief when another couple crossed from the opposite side and began walking in front of them in the direction of the exit just ahead. Somehow, the sight of other people nearby helped to ease her apprehension.

"I suppose we might as well go back. There's no sign of her." Even as she spoke, Jennifer continued to scan their surroundings. Something hovered at the edge of her memory, something about Whitney, standing on the corner, innocently watching that clown. . . .

"Daniel," she said abruptly, "that clown Whitney was so taken with—what if—"

Her words died into the darkness as a scream pierced the night.

The man and woman ahead of them came to a sharp halt. Sunny began to bark furiously, straining at her harness, and Daniel turned toward Jennifer as if waiting for an explanation. Before she could tell him anything, however, another cry rang out.

The other couple took off at a run, in the direction of the alley that ran between the bank building and Taylor's shoe store. Behind them, Jennifer kept her hand locked on Daniel's arm to guide him as they, too, began to run.

The other couple stopped for only an instant at the entrance to the alley, then went on. *"You—"* the man shouted. "What are you doing? Get away from her!"

As they turned into the alley, Jennifer stumbled over a loose piece of old paving brick but kept on going, Daniel beside her. Only a pale ribbon of light from the moon overhead filtered down between the buildings, but Jennifer could see a shadowed figure slumped at the far end of the alley. The couple ahead blocked her view, but only for an instant. Heart pounding, her chest on fire, Jennifer recognized the fallen figure, realized who it was at the same moment she saw the flash of white looming over her.

Jennifer screamed and the clown's head shot up, his grotesque white face a startled rictus. Then he turned and bolted from the alley, disappearing into the night.

"Whitney! Oh, Daniel—it's Whitney! I think she's hurt!"

By the time they reached Whitney, she had coiled herself against the side of the building, pushing her face and hands against the stone, as if trying to melt into it. She was shaking violently, gasping for breath.

Jennifer dropped down beside her, putting a hand to her shoulder. Whitney jerked and tried to scramble away, flailing her hands as if to ward off an attacker. Jennifer reached for her, pressing close enough that Whitney finally recognized her. With a choked sob, she collapsed into Jennifer's arms.

Jennifer held her, waiting, murmuring to Daniel so he would know what was happening. Finally, when the trembling had subsided, she drew back just enough for Whitney to read her lips. "What happened?" she asked the obviously terrified Whitney. "Are you hurt?"

For a moment Whitney merely stared at her through glazed eyes.

"Whitney? Are you all right?"

Finally, Whitney's gaze cleared. She blinked, started to speak, instead nodded in reply.

Jennifer was vaguely aware of the other couple telling Daniel they would go for the police. She held Whitney for a long time, feeling the other's frailness as she continued to tremble against Jennifer's shoulder.

At last, Whitney stirred and slowly eased away. "How did you . . . find me?" she asked, signing the words as she spoke.

"We heard you scream."

Whitney looked surprised. "You heard me?" she asked softly. "I wasn't sure I actually . . . screamed out loud. . . . I was so frightened. . . ."

Jennifer reached to give her friend a reassuring hug, then stopped when she noticed a dark bruise spreading across Whitney's cheekbone, just beneath her eye. "Whitney—your face! He *hit* you!"

The look Whitney turned on her as she lifted her hand to her cheek made Jennifer flinch. Whitney's eyes held the terror-filled, hunted look of a victim. But there was something else, an evasive, almost furtive, expression.

Shaken, Jennifer moved to get a closer look at her friend's face, drawing back when Whitney quickly turned away.

"Jennifer?" Daniel's voice reminded her that he had no way of knowing what was going on.

"Her face is bruised," she told him, her voice low as she continued to watch Whitney. "It looks as if she's taken a hard blow."

Anger darkened Daniel's features. "Do you think she needs a doctor? I can call Dad."

Jennifer turned back to Whitney, touching her lightly on the arm to get her attention. "Whitney, Daniel wants to know if you want to see a doctor. We'll call Lucas if—"

Without letting her finish, Whitney quickly shook her head in protest. "No! No," she repeated in a more controlled tone of voice. "I'm . . . fine. I just want . . . to go home."

"We have to wait for the police," Daniel reminded her gently.

Whitney, watching him closely to read his lips, nodded reluctantly. Leaning on Jennifer, she pulled herself to her feet. For an instant she weaved, and Jennifer was afraid she was going to fall. But with one hand against the stone wall, she straightened, waiting, as if to clear her head, before turning back to Jennifer with an uncertain smile.

"I'm all right, Jennifer. Don't . . . worry."

"Whitney?"

At Daniel's questioning tone, Jennifer gestured to Whitney to turn toward him, so she could read his lips.

"Whitney, do you have any idea at all who did this?"

"Daniel," Jennifer put in, "it was the clown—the Pierrot! He was right here standing over her! He ran when he saw us coming."

Daniel pulled in a deep breath, letting it out slowly. "Do you know if he had a weapon of any kind, Whitney? A gun, a knife—"

Again Whitney shook her head. "I didn't . . . see anything."

Searching her expression closely, Jennifer asked, "Whitney, do you have any idea why he attacked you?"

She saw something unreadable flicker in Whitney's eyes. "I tried to run," she said woodenly. "He was trying to take me . . . away, to take me . . . with him."

Chilled by Whitney's quiet, emotionless statement, Jennifer stared at her. "You think he was trying to—abduct you?"

Whitney's only answer was to nod and look away.

Jennifer would have pressed, but Daniel touched her arm. "Jennifer, she's had quite a scare, and the police will want to question her. Maybe you'd better give it a rest for now."

Jennifer looked from Daniel to Whitney, reluctantly conceding that he was probably right.

Whitney lay sleepless in the Kaines' guest room most of the night. She had tried to resist Jennifer's insistence that she stay with them, but the truth was that she had been too frightened to spend the night alone in her own house.

Turning toward the window, she stared at the moon-dusted grove of pine trees outside. Her hand plucked nervously at the bedcovers, her head spinning with possibilities, all of them terrifying.

With a soft moan of frustration, she clenched her teeth, willing her mind to shut out the tormenting memories. Her body was rigid with tension.

She didn't dare sleep. Not tonight. The dreams would come—the nightmares and the raw agonizing fear that always accompanied them. Up until tonight, she had thought she had finally conquered the fear, at least the worst of it. The ugly dreams no longer tortured her. The pain no longer pursued her through sleepless hours night after night.

It had taken months, but at last she had begun to feel secure with her hard-won freedom from terror. Little by little she was learning to rely on the presence and the protection of the Lord.

But tonight, if she slept, the dreams would come again.

Please, Lord, please help me to stop thinking about it . . . please. . . .

It wasn't the same as the other time. Of course it wasn't. It was just some local creep trying to have a little sick fun at her expense. Most likely, he had been drunk. He probably hadn't even known who she was. She had simply happened along at the wrong time, that's all. He'd been out to terrorize someone . . . anyone.

She tossed restlessly, turning over and burying her face in the pillow.

It's over. I wasn't hurt. Nothing really happened. Nothing is going to happen. It can't. It can't possibly happen again. . . . Oh, Lord, you wouldn't let it happen again, would you? Not again . . .

THREE

O UT of control, he hurled the clown suit across the room. The pants and tunic billowed to the floor like black-and-white sails ripped from their mast.
He stood, unmoving, staring at the suit. His face felt tight and hot, as much from anger as exertion. Whirling around, he howled savagely into the empty room, punching the wall with his fist.

"I should have *waited!*" Rage thundered inside his head, pounded behind his eyes. "Why didn't I *wait?*"

After a moment, he crossed the room and picked up the clown suit, dangling it from his fingers for an instant before tossing it onto the bed. Finally, he sank down beside it, splayed both hands on his knees, and sat staring through the doorway into the kitchen.

Rubbing both knees, he willed his body to wind down from the rage that threatened to blind him with its intensity.

"So close," he muttered, his voice dropping abruptly. "I was so close."

He began to rock back and forth on the edge of the bed, slowly and rhythmically. As he rocked, his breathing slowed, the flushed heat in his face dissipated, and his eyes began to clear.

Finally, he ceased rocking. He glanced down at himself with surprise, only now aware that he was clammy and uncomfortable.

The knit shirt and corduroy pants he'd been wearing beneath the clown suit were drenched with perspiration.

He curled his mouth with distaste. Anxious to be rid of the offensive clothing, he nevertheless shivered at the thought of bathing again. The rooms were cold, and he was tired. So tired. He needed to rest, longed to crawl into bed and sleep for hours.

But in order to sleep, he had to be clean.

He rose from the bed and picked up the clown suit, this time handling it more carefully. He folded it and put it into the suitcase with its mate.

Straightening, he glanced around the room until he spied the black cap and white gloves just inside the doorway, where he had tossed them in the heat of his anger. He retrieved them, placing them in the suitcase on top of the clown suits.

"Next time," he said softly, staring down at the open suitcase. "Next time will be different. I won't lose you again, Whitney-love."

He walked into the kitchen and caught a glimpse of himself in the shaving mirror on the table. Stopping, he postured, contorting his paint-smeared face into a self-mocking parody of a smiling clown.

Abruptly, he frowned, his mood darkening. He had gotten careless tonight. Impatient and careless. Seeing her so close, touching her, had made him lose control, made him reckless.

He should have been patient, should have waited. His intention had been simply to watch her, perhaps tease her a little, even frighten her. But nothing else. Not yet. The nearness of her had undone him. Now she would be on guard, the very thing he didn't want.

He began to pull at the knuckles of first one hand, then the other, weaving the upper half of his body sideways as he kneaded his fingers.

Those people she had been with—the blind man and the woman—where did they fit into her life? He knew about the Kaines, of course. He had been trailing Whitney's every move for days, watching where she went, what she did. Sometimes she went to the radio station; occasionally she had lunch with the Kaines. Three nights ago she had been at their house until after eleven.

He didn't like that. He had hoped to find her entirely on her own, not getting tight with a couple of meddling do-gooders.

He would deal with them if he had to.

From this point on, he would plan every move, every detail. He would take it slow, be careful. Extremely careful. First he would unnerve her, throw her off balance, shake her up a little. Then he could move in and start putting on the pressure.

That was the part he liked best, the first act. Watching them come unglued. It gave more drama to the play, made the ending far more interesting.

With the others, it had been only repeats of the same old scenario: first punishment, followed by justice, then the final cleansing. But for Whitney it would be different. True, the ending would be the same, but a whole new act would have to be written just for her. A new and different act that would balance the entire performance.

This time it was about revenge.

FOUR

B Y Monday, things were back to normal, at least on the surface.

The board meeting of the Friend-to-Friend Association was held that morning in the station's conference room, just as it was every month. Except for a little under-standable tension, Jennifer thought Whitney seemed remarkably composed throughout the meeting. Her suggestions were con-structive, her comments clear and intelligent, as always. Her eyes, however, were smudged with shadows, and her complexion was unhealthily pale, as if she hadn't slept well for days.

After staying Friday night with the Kaines, Whitney had spent the remainder of the weekend at her own home, despite Jennifer's pro-tests. They had talked for a few minutes after church Sunday, only long enough for Whitney to report that the police had no new leads on her assailant. Jennifer had sensed a new restraint about Whitney, or at least a subtle deepening of her usual reserve. Still, Daniel had said that any change right now was to be expected, and Jennifer sup-posed he was right; she could only hope it was temporary.

The three of them had planned to have lunch together after the meeting today, and Jennifer was looking forward to it. Shortly after they left the conference room, however, Daniel stopped her in the hallway. "Why don't you and Whitney go to lunch alone? Just the two of you."

"But I thought you wanted to come, too."

"I do, but I've got a time problem this afternoon. Besides," he said, thrusting one hand into his pocket as they walked down the hall, "it might be better if the two of you had some time alone together. Whitney sounds to me as if she's strung pretty tight right now."

Jennifer sighed. "She is. But what are you going to do about lunch?"

"I had a call early this morning from a fellow who wants to talk with me. I told him to come by about eleven-thirty." He stopped with Sunny at the door to Jennifer's office. "I'm doing Gabe's news and the one-thirty *Contact* show for the next two weeks while he and Lyss are in Huntington, so I thought if you don't mind, I'd talk with Devlin over lunch. I don't have any other free time today."

"Devlin?"

He nodded. "Michael Devlin. Says he's a photojournalist."

"What in the world is a photojournalist doing in Shepherd Valley?" She reached up to straighten the collar of Daniel's shirt under his crewneck sweater. "And what does he want to talk with you about?"

He shrugged, lifting his chin while she worked on his collar. "He said someone referred him to me for information on the community."

"You've never heard of him?"

"No, I guess he's been in town only a couple of days." Daniel smiled as she pressed his collar into place and kissed him lightly on the cheek. "He has an accent of some sort—Irish, maybe— I'm not sure." He touched the face of his Braille watch. "He should be here soon."

"All right. Whitney and I will go on, then, so I can get back in case you need me later."

"I always need you."

"See that it stays that way."

"I think I'd like another kiss, please."

"You're a greedy man, Daniel Kaine." She raised her face for his kiss.

"Nope," he corrected her afterward. "Just a man who's in love with his wife. See you later, darlin'. I'm going down to the studio; Lee wants me to jock the last half of the hour with him."

She watched him, smiling as he turned and walked down the hall with Sunny.

Back at her desk, Jennifer made a minor adjustment in the last quarter hour of the chart for her afternoon show, then thumbed through her messages. She decided anything else could wait until after lunch and got up, activating her voice mail before leaving the office to meet Whitney.

At the end of the hall, she stopped just short of the door to the lobby. A stranger was standing at the reception desk, facing the glass-enclosed broadcasting studio. She could see only his profile, but it was probably safe to assume that he was the man Daniel had told her about; unfamiliar faces were rare in Shepherd Valley. No doubt this would be Michael Devlin.

Dressed simply in a black bomber jacket and jeans, he looked harmless enough. He was tall, lean-faced, wiry, and obviously fit. His burnished complexion appeared slightly wind-whipped. His hair, thick and carelessly tousled, was a peculiar shade of rich, dark mahogany just beginning to silver at the temples. Strong features evoked a hint of stubbornness, while a mouth bracketed by two deep lines created a somewhat cynical expression.

His eyes when he turned to Jennifer were brooding and sharply watchful. She caught a sensation of a panther, stealthy and restless, with a barely controlled energy that threatened to explode at any moment.

As if judging her to be of no importance, he turned his attention back to the studio without so much as a change in expression.

Jennifer walked the rest of the way into the lobby. Only then, seeing the direction of his gaze, did she realize that Whitney, not the studio, was the subject of his attention. With her back turned to the reception desk, Whitney stood watching Daniel and Lee Kelsey through the studio window; she was obviously unaware of anyone else's presence in the room.

Jennifer cleared her throat. "May I help you?"

At that moment Whitney caught a glimpse of Jennifer out of the corner of her eye and spun around.

At the sight of Whitney's face, the stranger seemed to freeze. After a moment, still looking slightly stunned, he nudged the strap of a large camera bag a little higher on his shoulder and said, "I'd like to see Daniel Kaine, please."

A blunt, precise edge hardened what might otherwise have been a pleasing voice. As Daniel had indicated, his caller had an accent, a soft but distinct lilt.

"You're Mr. Devlin?" Jennifer asked.

"I am, yes."

"I'm Jennifer Kaine, Daniel's wife." She glanced into the studio to see that Daniel still had on his headset. "Daniel is just finishing up a program. He should be off the air in a moment."

Devlin had already turned his attention back to Whitney, who was studying him intently and with some bewilderment.

Jennifer hesitated, watching them, then made a brief introduction.

Immediately, Devlin's expression seemed to gentle. "Miss Sharyn," he said, "I'm very happy to meet you."

Whitney frowned, lifted a restraining hand to him, then touched her lips and shook her head to show Devlin she didn't understand.

"Whitney is deaf," Jennifer explained quickly. "If you could speak more slowly, it might help." She paused. "I think it's your accent. Whitney's an expert lip-reader, but it may take her a moment to get used to you."

He glanced from Jennifer to Whitney, his expression softening even more as he repeated his greeting, enunciating his words more distinctly this time.

Whitney gave him a shy smile and offered her hand. "I'm . . . glad to meet you."

Jennifer watched in silence as Devlin pressed his fingers around Whitney's outstretched hand. The transformation in the man was amazing. Gone was the grim-faced stranger. In his place stood an unexpectedly pleasant-featured man with a boyish smile and the formidable charm of a Celtic prince.

Like most men meeting Whitney for the first time, Devlin seemed to find it difficult to tear his gaze away from her. Jennifer wasn't surprised. From the beginning, the new director of Friend-to-Friend had reminded her of an exquisitely perfect porcelain figurine.

Everything about Whitney Sharyn was delicate, feminine, and achingly lovely. Her beauty was sweetly elegant rather than dramatic or sensational.

Jennifer folded her arms and watched Michael Devlin's protective armor drop away and melt at his feet.

She couldn't help but wonder how much longer he might have drawn out what should have been a simple handshake if Daniel and Sunny hadn't come out of the studio at that moment.

"Jennifer, did Glenn McDonald call back yet?" Holding Sunny's harness with one hand while he smoothed his dark hair with the other, he stopped just short of the reception desk.

"No, not unless he called during the meeting," she told him. "But Katharine didn't leave a note. Daniel—"

"Would you try him again? There's still a bad short in that

number two suspension mike. I'm beginning to feel as though I'm sitting in the electric chair every time it's open."

"I'll call him right away. Daniel—"

"And make sure he knows it hasn't been right since he was here last week. I'm not going to pay him until he gets it fixed."

"I'll tell him. Daniel—"

"If I'm going to get electrocuted, I'd just as soon not make it a live performance." He paused. "I thought you and Whitney were going to lunch."

"We are, but—"

"Good. I thought Devlin would be here by now. I'm not going to have much time."

"Daniel—"

"What?"

"He *is* here," Jennifer said. "Mr. Devlin is here, at the desk."

"Oh. Why didn't you tell me?" he asked mildly.

Jennifer looked at him. After a long sigh, she introduced the two men.

Dropping Sunny's harness, Daniel inclined his head and extended his hand, waiting for Devlin to take it.

Jennifer watched as Devlin's eyes flicked from Daniel's face to the harnessed retriever at his side. Understanding quickly dawned in his expression.

"Mr. Kaine," he said, his tone friendly, his gaze intent as he shook Daniel's hand. "I was referred to you by a fellow over at the Commerce Office—Robinson. I'm interested in gathering some information on your community. He said you might be willing to help me."

Daniel nodded, releasing Devlin's hand. "You said on the phone that you're a journalist?"

"A photojournalist, actually. I'm doing a series of features on small Appalachian communities like your own."

"Sounds interesting. Where are you from, Mr. Devlin?"

"Michael, please," Devlin offered. "Or Dev—I answer to either. I'm from Cincinnati most recently. Belfast before that."

"Belfast—as in Ireland?"

"Northern Ireland, yes, that's right."

Jennifer noticed that while Devlin was carrying on the conversation with Daniel, his glance continued to dart to and from Whitney. Inexplicably, she recalled a line from a play. . . . *"A man walks out of the shadows, a dark man of secrets and night. . . ."*

She pushed the thought away as Daniel and Devlin went on talking. "Hal Robinson makes me sound like the local historian," Daniel said lightly, "which I'm not. But if you'd like to have lunch, I'll try to answer whatever questions I can for you."

"Lunch? Today, do you mean?"

"Yes, in a few minutes. I have a news broadcast to do at one o'clock, so I'll need to be back by then. There's a great little restaurant nearby, just down the hill."

Devlin appeared to be caught short by Daniel's friendliness, but he quickly recovered. "I'd like that. I haven't eaten yet today."

"You said you've only been in town a couple of days," Daniel said. "Where are you staying?"

"I'm at a motel across town right now. The, ah, Covered Bridge—"

He broke off at Daniel's soft chuckle. "Would I be correct in assuming you'd like to find a room with a few more conveniences?"

Devlin gave a short laugh. "Actually, I'd be content with hot water." He pulled a small piece of notepaper out of his jacket pocket and glanced at it. "I've been checking the listings in the newspaper. There are two or three here that sound promising. Perhaps you could give me an idea where they are. There's one on Lee Street and another on Greenbrier Court."

Apparently Whitney had been following Devlin's speech carefully. She answered before Daniel could. "That's . . . my street," she said, her words coming slowly but clearly.

Devlin studied her. With what appeared to be a conscious effort to speak more clearly for her benefit, he asked, "Greenbrier Court? That's where you live?"

Whitney nodded, signing as she spoke. "And work. My . . . apartment is in back of the office."

Devlin's piercing stare measured Whitney with unhurried thoroughness until Daniel's voice interrupted.

"Greenbrier's a nice street. Mostly renovated older homes and a few small business offices. It's a better area than Lee Street," he mused. "Nothing much there except some cramped one-room efficiencies."

"Then I'll try Greenbrier first," Devlin said brusquely. "I can't do with an efficiency; I need some extra space I can convert to a temporary darkroom, you see."

"You make your own prints?" asked Daniel.

Devlin nodded, then caught himself. "I do, yes."

Adjusting the camera bag on his shoulder, he turned to Whitney. "Are you a native of the area, Miss Sharyn?"

Whitney gave him a faint smile and shook her head. "I've only been here for . . . three months."

His low-set brows arched. "I don't suppose you'd be free to direct me to your neighborhood later?"

When Whitney explained that she had plans for lunch and appointments scheduled for the entire afternoon, Jennifer drew a small breath of relief. She supposed her guardedness about Devlin was reasonable enough: after Whitney's recent ordeal, *any* stranger would be suspect, at least in a small community like Shepherd Valley. Devlin had a hard edge about him, a remoteness that didn't quite mesh with his obvious interest in Whitney.

For once, she was almost grateful for the reserve Whitney displayed around most men—a reserve that at times almost seemed to border on fearfulness. Jennifer found herself hoping that her friend would maintain that aloofness around Michael Devlin, at least for now.

"Daniel, I wonder if you've a washroom close by?" Devlin asked. "I drove out earlier this morning to get some shots of the valley, and I'd like to dust myself off a bit before lunch."

"Down the hall to your right," Daniel told him, inclining his head.

With another covert glance at Whitney, Devlin left the lobby.

After a moment, Daniel turned to Jennifer and Whitney. "How about that? Our little town may end up making a national magazine."

He didn't seem to notice Jennifer's lack of response but went on. "So—what does he look like? He sounds young."

Jennifer answered almost automatically. "Early thirties, I imagine. Tall, trim, dark hair."

"That's vague enough," Daniel quipped.

Jennifer looked at him. "He's . . . difficult to describe. There's something about him. . . ."

"Uh-oh," Daniel said, grinning. "Here comes the character study."

Jennifer ignored him. "He's . . . aloof," she finally said.

"Aloof?" Daniel lifted a dark eyebrow.

"Aloof," Jennifer repeated. "And perhaps a little angry. I don't know that he's a man I'd trust."

At Daniel's puzzled expression, Jennifer shot a questioning glance at Whitney, who had been reading their lips intently.

Whitney met her look with a small, uncertain nod of agreement, her gaze going to the hallway door where Devlin had just exited. "He has pain . . . in his eyes, though. Did you see?" she said, her voice soft.

Surprised, Jennifer found herself again hoping that Whitney wouldn't suddenly discard her usual caution around men. Especially around *this* man.

FIVE

Y OU did *what?*"

Jennifer leaned forward, pressing the palms of both hands on top of Daniel's desk as she stared at him with disbelief. The late afternoon sun spilled through the open drapes of the window behind him, framing his head and shoulders in an intense golden glow. As if surprised by her reaction, he knit his brows together in a small frown. "I invited him to the house for pizza Wednesday night," he repeated mildly.

"Why on earth would you do that, Daniel?" Jennifer leaned even farther over his desk. "You just met Michael Devlin this morning. The man is a stranger to us."

With infuriating calm, Daniel steepled his fingers together to support his chin. "I invited him for pizza, Jennifer. I didn't ask him to move in."

"Still—"

"He's new in town," he reminded her patiently, much in the same tone of voice he sometimes used with Jason. "He doesn't know anyone except us, and I thought it would be a nice gesture."

"Didn't you remember that we've already asked Whitney to come home with us after prayer meeting?"

"I remembered," he said casually. "Why? Do you think she'll mind?"

Would she mind? Jennifer wasn't sure. "What if *I* mind?"

Movement from Sunny, lying next to Daniel's chair, caught her attention. The retriever, head raised, ears pricked, regarded her with troubled eyes. The dog whimpered softly, and Jennifer felt a pinch of guilt; her tone must have been sharper than she'd intended.

Daniel's expression cleared, and he smiled a little. "Maybe you'd feel better about Devlin if I told you something I learned while we were at lunch."

Immediately interested, Jennifer sank down in the chair across from his desk. "I'm listening."

Locking his hands comfortably behind his head, Daniel leaned back in the worn, oversized leather chair that had served his grandfather, the station's founder, for years before Daniel had inherited both the chair and the station.

"Devlin's an ex-cop," he said easily, propping one large foot on the top of his desk.

"A *police officer?*" Jennifer stared at him blankly.

Daniel nodded. "In Belfast."

Still suspicious, Jennifer considered this unexpected bit of information. "Did he say why he left?"

He shrugged. "Not really. He mentioned something about the violence. The 'troubles,' I believe he called it."

"And of course you didn't try to learn anything more than what he volunteered."

A ghost of a smile scurried across his features. "I'm afraid not."

Jennifer squirmed a little at the thought that a part of her didn't really want to hear any redeeming information about Devlin. Even so, she couldn't resist one more question. "He's made a rather drastic change in career direction, hasn't he? From a policeman to a freelance photojournalist, or whatever he says he is."

Shaking his head, Daniel laughed. "You never quit, do you?"

"Well, I would have asked more questions than I'm sure *you* did," Jennifer countered.

"Oh, I don't doubt that for a minute, darlin'."

"So all you really know about Michael Devlin is that he's someone who *says* he used to be a police officer, who now goes around taking pictures and writing stories."

Jennifer had seen that long-suffering, groping-for-patience smile at various times in their relationship and was wholly undaunted by it. "Well?" she pressed.

A flash of mischief darted across his face. "At this point, I don't know much more than the fact that he uses a good aftershave, doesn't smoke, and doesn't seem to crack his knuckles or grind his teeth. At least not that I noticed."

Jennifer made a sound of disgust.

He ignored her. "Devlin is apparently doing some kind of a special series on Appalachian settlements. Said he'd be in the area a few weeks, taking pictures, interviewing people, sniffing out some human-interest stories—that sort of thing." He stretched. "That's about it. That, and the fact that he's coming to our house for pizza Wednesday night."

Jennifer leaned forward. "Since he's going to eat with us, I assume he's going to church with us, too?"

Daniel dropped his hands from behind his head and rested them on the chair arms, then lowered his foot from the desk back to the floor. "He is," he answered somewhat hesitantly, "but to be honest, I got the feeling he agreed to go only when he found out Whitney would be there."

"That wouldn't surprise me at all," Jennifer snapped, "considering the fact that he couldn't tear his eyes away from her in the lobby this morning!" She broke off, then added, "I wonder if he's even a Christian."

Daniel's answer wasn't what she expected. "Yes, he is. The conversation about Wednesday night's prayer meeting brought up the subject," he explained. "But I got the distinct impression that he didn't want to talk about it."

Neither of them spoke for a moment. Finally Daniel tipped his head and patted the arm of the chair. "Come here," he said quietly.

Jennifer got up and walked around the desk, stopping for a moment to rub Sunny's ears before perching on the arm of Daniel's chair. "Don't be cross with me, Daniel," she said. "I can't help it if I don't trust this man. I can't help worrying about Whitney. You know how much I like her."

"You worry too much," he told her, taking her hand. "And I don't understand your suspicions about Devlin. Can't you just give the guy a chance?"

His question made Jennifer stop and think. "I suppose I'm frightened," she told him.

Daniel frowned. "Frightened? For Whitney?"

Jennifer nodded to herself. "It's not just Michael Devlin," she said. "I don't think I'd be able to trust *any* stranger right now. Daniel, hasn't it at least occurred to you that Devlin could be the man who attacked Whitney the other night?"

His expression sobered. "I've thought of it," he admitted, squeezing her hand. "But *anyone* could have been wearing that clown suit, Jennifer. There's no reason to assume it was a stranger."

He was right, of course. But it was much easier to suspect a stranger than someone they might know. "Did you mention the attack on Whitney to Devlin?" she asked him.

He nodded. "We talked about it."

"How did he react?"

Daniel didn't answer right away. "He sounded genuinely outraged," he finally said. "But I can tell you, this isn't a man who says much about what he thinks—or feels. He's—" He stopped, as if struggling to find the right word.

"Aloof," Jennifer supplied.

"No, I don't think so. Not exactly. I got the impression of a man who's very self-controlled, possibly even a little awkward around strangers himself." He paused, then went on. "Jennifer, you believe the attack on Whitney was something planned, don't you? A personal assault."

Jennifer studied him. "Don't *you?*"

He shrugged. "Not necessarily. Whitney might simply have been in the wrong place at the wrong time. The man who jumped her might not have even known her name. Some of these creeps are just out there looking for a woman to terrorize—*any* woman."

Jennifer considered the possibility. If he was right, if it had been a random assault, then the danger might be over.

At least for Whitney.

She was a little surprised to realize how much she hoped he *was* right. The idea of Whitney's being singled out by an assailant for *any* reason was even more terrifying than an unpremeditated attack.

She looked at him. "We've spent a lot of time discussing *my* feelings about Michael Devlin. What about *yours?* You're the one who had lunch with him. How do *you* feel about him?"

"You don't get to know much about a person in an hour. But at this point, I'd have to say that I found myself liking the man."

"But, Daniel, you don't *know* him!"

He lifted one dark brow. "Neither do you," he said evenly, "but it seems to me you've made up your mind *not* to like him."

Jennifer winced at the justified rebuke.

"You asked me how I feel about Devlin," Daniel went on, his tone thoughtful. "At first he comes across as rather hard, but I imagine that's fairly typical of a police officer. Beyond that, though, I get a sense of a man who's keenly intelligent and very professional. I'll just bet Devlin is good at what he does." He paused. "I have a hunch he's a loner . . . and maybe a little cynical."

He shifted in his chair. "I also think he's an interesting fellow, and I'd like to know him better."

Jennifer studied Daniel for a moment. "I'm still not comfortable with having him over so soon—especially if he's only interested in being with Whitney."

Daniel lifted both hands in a palms-up gesture of hopelessness. "Did I say *Devlin* is hard?" He chuckled then and pulled her onto his lap.

"Daniel, someone might come in!"

Ignoring her protest, he drew her into his arms. "In case you've forgotten, we're married. That makes it perfectly acceptable behavior for you to sit on my lap."

"Katharine—"

"—is already gone for the day." He kissed her lightly, tightening his embrace even more.

"Mm." Enjoying the closeness and the warm fortress of his powerful arms, Jennifer stroked her cheek against his sweater. Her weak protest came out as a purr. "Still, someone could walk in."

"No one's here but us." He kissed her again.

Jennifer allowed herself one more moment of closeness before drawing back and prodding his chest with a stern finger. "Daniel, I want you to promise me that you'll be careful. About Devlin. You won't—trust him too much too quickly, will you? For Whitney's sake?"

Laughing, he tapped her gently on the end of her nose. "My sweet Jennifer, you are absolutely impossible. You just can't resist a sad-eyed stray or a lost soul, can you?"

"Well, I'm afraid I can't always be as effective as I'd like to be with lost souls," she admitted with a sigh, "but I guess I *am* a pushover for a sad-eyed stray."

Clasping both of her shoulders, he pushed her gently from his lap as he got to his feet. "Is that why you married me?"

"Of course not. I married you because you're a devastating man."

"Yeah?" His grin was pleased, if a little foolish. He put his arms around her waist and drew her closer. "Devastating, huh?"

"Oh, yes. Definitely devastating."

Seemingly satisfied with her assurance, he nodded. "Was that the only reason?"

"Well, no. Actually, there was one other thing."

He dropped his hands away from her waist, waiting. "And what, exactly, was that?"

"Job security." She flicked a piece of red sweater fuzz—her own—from his shoulder as she touched a light kiss to his bearded cheek. "A woman has to be practical, you know."

"Oh, absolutely," he agreed, sliding an arm around her shoulder as they started out of the office. "It's a jungle out there."

SIX

W HITNEY felt a light touch on her arm as she stepped onto the porch. She turned to find Jennifer, who had followed her outside.

"Why don't you just stay here tonight?" Jennifer urged. "It's late, and I'd feel so much better—"

"If you could keep an eye on me," Whitney finished with an affectionate grin. "Stop worrying about me. I'm fine."

Jennifer hugged her, then held her at arm's length to study her face. "How do you think the evening went?"

"Very well," Whitney assured her, signing as she spoke. "You only insulted . . . Michael Devlin once or twice. I'm five pounds heavier, . . . thanks to Daniel's pizza. And Jason got to stay up an extra hour. Sounds like a successful evening to me."

Jennifer wrinkled her nose. "Jason spent most of his extra hour shadowing Devlin. He certainly seemed to take a liking to the man, did you notice?"

Whitney nodded. "I think he liked Jason, too, letting him use that expensive-looking camera to take pictures of Sunny."

"I have to admit he turned out to be a lot more personable than I expected," Jennifer answered. "You could almost say he was good company, if you wanted to be generous." She cocked her head to one side and subjected Whitney to a thorough examination. "So what do *you* think of Devlin?"

"I think," Whitney said, lifting her eyebrows, "that the poor man . . . had better watch his back around you."

"Are you being evasive?"

"With you?" Whitney laughed. "I wouldn't even try." She gave Jennifer a friendly pat on the shoulder. "I *do* have to go. Thanks again for everything."

Jennifer managed one more parting shot before Whitney could step off the porch. "He's interested in you, you know. He hardly took his eyes off you all evening."

Flustered, Whitney tried to ignore the unexpected thud of her heart at Jennifer's statement. Forcing another smile, she said a hasty good night and turned to go before Jennifer could stop her.

As she backed out of the driveway and started down the hill, Whitney realized that Jennifer's comment about Michael Devlin had shaken her more than she cared to admit. Especially in light of her inexplicable response to the man.

It was rare—extremely rare—for her to slip into a casual conversation with a man she scarcely knew. Yet tonight she had been able to do just that with Michael Devlin. For some reason, she had let her guard down around the Irish journalist, had even been comfortable with him. At least more comfortable than she would have thought possible, considering her usual distrust of strangers.

As she approached the bottom of the hill, she flipped on the heater, shivering at the blast of cold air that rushed out at her. She stopped, checked the intersection, then turned onto Keystone Drive.

Devlin is *a former policeman,* she reminded herself. Did that give him a little more credibility in her eyes?

Probably. Odd how much easier she found it to imagine the restless, wary-eyed Devlin as a police officer than as a nomadic, freelance photographer. His hard, cynical appearance, his almost abrasive directness, and his obvious physical power gave him an air of authority. Whitney thought he must have made a formidable opponent for any criminal.

He had been surprisingly gentle with *her,* though, she mused, recalling his unmistakable attempts throughout the evening to put her at ease. There had been only one bad moment, when he had unknowingly moved from an innocent conversation about her deafness into a part of her life Whitney refused to discuss with anyone, even Jennifer.

Daniel had gone to hear Jason's bedtime prayers while Jennifer made fresh coffee. Whitney had been sitting on the couch, staring at a thick log blazing in the fireplace, when Devlin walked over to the hearth.

Turning his back to the fire, he pushed his hands into his pockets and stood, openly studying her.

"Daniel tells me you've been deaf since you were a child," he said bluntly. "How is it that you can speak so clearly?"

"I didn't lose my . . . hearing until I was five," she answered, signing the words as she said them. "By that time, I had stored a lot of . . . audible speech memory."

He nodded, watching her intently. "Do you mind talking about it?"

She shook her head. "No. What I mind is for people to deliberately *avoid* talking about it." She was comfortable with his directness; in fact, she appreciated it. People usually found it difficult even to acknowledge her disability, much less question her about it.

"What caused it?" he asked. "Illness?"

"Meningitis," she replied, glancing into the fire for a moment before returning her attention to him.

He shifted his weight from one foot to the other, frowning. "You can't hear anything at all?"

"No. My residual hearing . . . wasn't enough to amplify."

"With a hearing aid, you mean?"

"That's right."

He looked down at the hearth, then back at her face. "I'm amazed at your lipreading ability, the way you keep up with the conversation going on around you."

Whitney set her coffee cup down on the table beside the couch. "I taught a class of deaf teenagers for three years," she told him, smiling at the memory. "I tried to make lipreading as much a priority as signing."

He came to sit down on the couch. "So—you're a teacher?"

Whitney shook her head. "Not . . . any lon-longer," she said, flinching at the halting stammer that suddenly gripped her. "When I still lived . . . in Louisville."

Why had she said that? She hadn't told anyone in Shepherd Valley where she was from except for Jennifer and Daniel.

"Louisville, Kentucky?" He smiled. "Well then, we weren't all that far away from each other, were we?"

Whitney frowned, then remembered that Devlin had mentioned living in Cincinnati after he arrived from Belfast.

"Did you relocate because of family?" he asked, apparently intent on steering the conversation back to her.

Whitney swallowed. "No," she said tightly. "I . . . took a new job." Briefly, she told him about the Friend-to-Friend Association.

"That must have been quite an adjustment for you."

Whitney looked at him.

"The change in lifestyles," he quickly qualified. "Moving from a city the size of Louisville into such a rural setting. Has it been difficult for you?"

Whitney relaxed a little. "Oh . . . no. No, not at all. I like it here . . . very much."

"Yes, it's a lovely place," he said, still watching her. He draped his arm along the back of the couch and smiled again. "I'm wondering if you'll allow me to spend some time with you, Miss Sharyn."

Whitney stiffened. As if he had seen her reaction, he went on to explain. "I'd like to visit your office sometime. I'm intrigued by the concept of the Association. It's rather a novel idea, isn't it? The disabled helping other disabled?"

Whitney drew a small breath of relief. "Yes . . . I suppose it is . . . or at least it used to be. Now there are a number of similar . . . organizations springing up throughout the country." She chose her words carefully as she went on. "You'd be welcome . . . to visit the office, of course. But I'm afraid you might be . . . disappointed. The actual work is done one-to-one, among the members. I'm just a coordinator."

"Still, I'd be interested," he insisted with a disarming smile. "Perhaps I can get you a bit of free publicity with one of my publications while I'm about it."

Whitney stared at him. "Publicity? No," she said quickly. "No, I don't think . . . we'd be interested in that."

He looked surprised. "I should think an organization like yours would welcome the exposure. It might help to generate additional donations."

"We don't depend on publicity for funding, Mr. Devlin—"

"Michael," he reminded her firmly, his eyes probing her gaze. "And publicity or not, I'd still like to spend a day with you at your office, if it wouldn't be too much bother."

To Whitney's enormous relief, Daniel returned just then, making it unnecessary for her to answer.

The rest of the evening had been pleasant enough, but in spite of Michael Devlin's irreproachable manners, he unnerved Whitney. In some unaccountable way, his presence triggered an edginess in her. She realized the feeling was something different from the distrust she often felt toward other men, but it unsettled her all the same.

It was his eyes, she thought, slowing for the caution light at Midmount and Keystone. A deep, brilliant green, they seemed to deflect all attention from his lean face; drawing others to him with the intensity of a magnetic field. More than once tonight she had been jolted by the irrational sensation that Michael Devlin *knew* her, knew everything about her.

In spite of its few tense moments, however, the evening seemed to have served as a turning point in restoring a measure of order and calm to her life. It was almost as if the night had provided a release from the anxiety and oppression triggered by the attack on Friday night.

Before tonight, Whitney had already caught herself sliding back into a self-enforced solitude—a solitude that had once become a virtual prison. But the companionship of her friends, and, in some strange way, the obvious interest of Michael Devlin, had acted as reminders that she didn't want—didn't *dare*—to return to her former isolation. She had wasted far too much time living in fear. She had buried herself alive in it. But not again. Now that she had finally gained the freedom from terror she had long sought, she was determined to hold on to it.

As terrifying as Friday night had been, she told herself, it was only a coincidence, nothing more. It had nothing to do with the other time. Friday night she had simply been a victim, not a . . . target, like before. She couldn't allow the horror of a moment to send her running away from life a second time.

Coming to the four-way stop at Jackson and Keystone, Whitney braked, then turned left onto Jackson Drive. Ever mindful of her inability to hear sirens or other traffic noise, she glanced in the rearview and side mirrors to check her surroundings. A solitary pair of headlights followed not too far behind. As she watched, the double beams of light moved up until they were within a car's length of her.

She kept one eye on the mirror as she drove. When the headlights continued to follow her all the way up Jackson Drive, Whitney felt her stomach clench. The darkness was thick, and it was late enough that there was no traffic and few house lights to be seen. As she approached the next intersection, she tapped the brake, looked both ways, then turned right onto Greenbrier. Her mouth went dry. The headlights in the rearview mirror were still with her.

Halfway up the block, however, the other vehicle slowed, then turned into a narrow alley that dissected Greenbrier on the left. With a shaky breath, Whitney relaxed against the back of the seat, easing her foot away from the gas pedal to slow her speed. She would soon be home.

Greenbrier Court was an old-money street with a turn-of-the-century elegance. Whitney never drove through the neighborhood without an almost proprietary sense of satisfaction. Rambling late-Victorian homes of brick, frame, and brownstone fronted the paved brick street, their broad double doors and precisely draped windows hinting of a quiet pride and stateliness, even in those structures that had been converted to apartments or professional offices.

As she pulled up in front of the enormous white-frame Gothic that housed the offices of Friend-to-Friend and her apartment, Whitney again glanced in the rearview mirror. Seeing nothing, she turned the engine off and pulled her keys from the ignition.

The house sat on an elevated bank, removed several feet from the street. She ran up the cracked cement steps, opened the wrought-iron gate, then hurried down the walk that bordered the left side of the house. A dim light glowed from the side porch at the rear, the entrance to her apartment.

She unlocked the door with one hand and fumbled for the wall switch with the other. Flipping on the light as she entered, she turned to close the door behind her.

Light from a frosted-glass globe overhead illuminated the entry, a wide hallway with worn carpet and dusty rose wallpaper. Quickly, she secured the push-button lock on the knob, then threw the bolt and security chain into place.

She stood just inside the door for a moment, her fingers resting lightly on its painted white surface. Fear washed over her at the very thought of entering the dark apartment, but pulling in a deep, steadying breath, she turned and shrugged out of her jacket.

Her gaze went to one of her few extravagances, a small legless desk with a high back full of pigeonholes that was securely fastened to the wall beside the coatrack. Then she started for the living room, dark beyond its open French doors. There was no overhead light, so she went to the table beside the couch and fumbled for the switch on the hand-painted lamp.

Standing perfectly still, she scanned the room. Whitney had sacrificed a certain amount of style for comfort. The two plump floral chairs by the fireplace were of no particular period, but she had bought them years before because the soft mauve-and-cream print appealed to her. The bookshelves behind the chairs held a wide variety of titles, including a few worn volumes of her favorite children's stories. She had left the heavy cream-toned drapes and lace undercurtains at the window.

Still edgy, she walked into the breakfast nook that joined the living room and kitchen. She turned on the overhead light, letting her gaze sweep the room as she removed the morning newspaper from the table. This was her favorite room in the house—the place she invariably came to when she wanted to sketch or write letters or simply sit by the large bay window and think.

With growing confidence, she walked into the kitchen, dropping the newspaper onto a stack of others beside the door. The room was large, far too spacious for her needs, but typical of the period. Modernization had been limited to fresh white paint, a freestanding stove and refrigerator, both white, and a good vinyl floor that was easy to clean.

Satisfied that everything was in order, Whitney crossed the narrow hall to the bathroom, which she gave only a cursory check, except for a sheepish glance behind the pink-and-white shower curtain.

Entering her bedroom, she crept carefully across the hardwood floor until she reached the edge of the hooked rug near the bed. The faint smell of fabric softener hovered about the room from the fresh linen she had just put on that morning. Her hand knocked against the glass bottom of the bedside lamp as she groped for the switch.

She was staring directly at the bed when she turned on the light, but at first she didn't see the grotesque figure sprawled in the middle of the comforter. Even when reality forced its way into her mind, she stood staring in blank disbelief for a full minute before uttering a choked cry.

The doll was at least two feet long, with a delicately slender body. The costume was monstrously correct: white pants, black-and-white tunic, complete with a fussy white ruff and a small black skullcap. The worst part was the face. Painted in clown white, its eyes were slashed with black; its mouth was a bloodred streak.

A Pierrot doll.

It lay flat on its back, staring up at her with a hideously evil smile. In its left hand lay one dead long-stemmed rose. The other hand held a knife, small but dreadfully authentic.

Bewilderment turned to terror. Whitney's chest burned. Her throat went numb. She began to shake so violently she thought her heart would explode. Still she couldn't force her eyes away from the doll.

The blinking light of her signaling system suddenly broke into the horror. Alerted that the TDD phone was ringing, Whitney whirled around, then turned back to the bed.

Unable to tear her gaze away from the doll, she backed up to the night table. Suddenly the lamp stopped flashing. She had waited too long.

Only then did she see the note lying beneath the doll's right hand.

With as much loathing as if she were picking up a copperhead, Whitney slipped the note out from under the cold porcelain hand, biting her lip to ward off hysteria.

She straightened and read the message through a blur of terror. . . .

> You weren't here when I came for you, Whitney-love. But that's all right. I'm leaving a gift for you, something to keep you company until I come back. Next time, I'll make sure you're at home before I come in. Wait for me, Whitney. I'll be back.

Whitney's legs started to buckle beneath her, and she grabbed at the night table to keep from falling. *It can't be.* . . .

With glazed eyes, she stood staring at the paper in her hand. Her throat filled with hot bile, and she began to shake her head furiously back and forth in denial.

No . . . it's not him. . . . It can't be him. . . . Oh, no, Lord, no . . .

Whitney shuddered, letting the note slip from her trembling hand and drift slowly to the floor. She started edging backward to the open doorway. Like a broken marionette, her legs jerked woodenly as she retreated.

Suddenly she stopped. *What if he was still in the apartment? Should I stay here in the bedroom and lock myself in?*

She froze. No. He couldn't be inside. She had gone through the entire apartment as soon as she came in. Besides, if she locked herself inside the bedroom, she had no way of knowing what was going on in the rest of the house. She couldn't hear. He could be anywhere . . . in the front office . . . upstairs.

She glanced up at the ceiling. All those vacant rooms on the second floor . . . nothing up there except supplies and old files. He could be up there . . . hiding . . . waiting.

But how did he get inside the house?

The doors had been locked when she left, she was sure, and still locked when she came home.

The office. She hadn't checked the office door. It could be standing wide open for all she knew. And the connecting door between the office and her apartment was a joke. The ancient, flimsy lock wouldn't have stopped a stray cat.

She covered her mouth with the back of her hand, choking back a scream.

Call Jennifer.

No, she couldn't. If it was—*him,* if he was back, she had to keep Jennifer and Daniel from finding out. It would be like it was before. Anyone who tried to help her would be in danger. She couldn't do that—*wouldn't* do that—to them.

What, then? She had to do *something.* She couldn't simply wait until he came for her.

Her mind rebelled against the thought. It couldn't possibly be him. They wouldn't have let him out. He was insane, dangerous. It had to be nothing more than a sick joke.

She would call the police.

She started toward the phone in the kitchen, then stopped. The police would ask her questions. They'd grill her, dig at her past, find out about the other time. Everyone would know. They wouldn't leave it alone, not after Friday night's attack.

Friday night.

It *had* been him. Not someone else. Not a horrible coincidence. Not a monstrous joke.

Cory.

Dear Lord, no. Please, no . . .

The lamp began to flash again, faster . . . faster.

Whitney whipped around to stare at the blinking light. It stopped, then started flashing again.

She looked from the lamp to the doll. Evil smiled back at her. *He was in the house!*

She had to get out. She bolted from the room, running down the narrow hall toward the front of the apartment.

At the back of her mind, she knew she should find a place to hide and stay there, stay quiet.

But he would find her. There *was* no place to hide. There had *never* been any place to hide.

She sprinted through the living room, fumbled with the chain, slid the bolt, twisted the knob.

Only when she threw open the door and saw him standing there, a dark and hulking silhouette looming in the doorway, did she realize that in the frenzy of her fear, she had made a terrible mistake.

The second sequence of flashing lights, rapid and in triple-time, wasn't the telephone alert. It was the signal for the doorbell.

SEVEN

S HE tried to squeeze past him, but he spread his arms to stop her. He caught her by the waist, trapping her.

Whitney exploded, slapping, punching, sobbing wildly as she struck at him.

He let go of her waist, grabbed both wrists with one hand, and held her. Taking a step inside the door, he forced her backward, into the light. The collar of his dark jacket was drawn up high around his neck. His face was a granite mask, set in a frown that could have issued from either anger or surprise.

Devlin!

He pushed her back another step, his eyes burning into hers. "Whitney—what's wrong?"

She tried to say his name, but she was paralyzed. Unable to catch a breath, she felt her head reel and the room begin to spin.

"Whitney! What is it? What's happened?"

She stared at him. *Devlin, not Cory . . .*

He watched her. His mouth was grim, his eyes on fire. Still holding her by the wrists, he kicked one leg out behind him and shut the door.

Slowly, he released her wrists and brought both hands up to grasp her firmly by the shoulders. Whitney shuddered, shrinking beneath his touch.

His eyes narrowed. "What's frightened you so? Whitney—"

Suddenly seized by a violent trembling, she looked away from him. Nausea clutched at her throat, and she swallowed down the taste of her own fear.

Devlin dropped one hand away from her shoulder, at the same time tightening his grasp on the other. Gently, he tipped her chin with his finger, making her face him.

"What's going on? Are you hurt?" Even as he spoke, he scanned their surroundings.

Whitney tried to answer, but her throat constricted, choking off her breath.

Devlin led her into the living room and eased her gently but firmly onto the couch, then sat down beside her.

Instinctively, Whitney drew back from him.

His frown deepened, but he made no attempt to touch her, instead waiting until she met his gaze. "Tell me," he said.

Whitney couldn't stop shaking. The temperature in the room seemed to be plummeting by the second.

Devlin retrieved a folded afghan from one of the fireside chairs, gently draped it around her shoulders, and resumed his seat next to her. "Better?"

Whitney clasped the afghan tightly to her and nodded.

After a moment Devlin shifted, dipping his head slightly to get her attention. "Tell me what happened."

Huddled under the afghan, Whitney tensed, looked away. She couldn't possibly tell him. She didn't even know him.

Forcing her voice, keeping her eyes cast down, she finally managed to speak. "Please . . . I . . . I can't."

Whitney could feel his eyes on her, but he said nothing.

At last she glanced up. Surprised, she saw that his expression appeared deeply concerned, even troubled.

"Whitney—" He stopped, then went on. "Why can't you tell me?"

Slowly, Whitney lifted her gaze from his lips to meet his eyes.
His look was steady—and unexpectedly kind.

It would be foolish to tell him. Even more foolish to trust him.
Besides, what could he do? What could *anyone* do?

"Whitney—I might be able to help, if you'd only trust me."

She shook her head. No one could help. She was living a night-mare from which she would never awaken. It was going to go on
forever.

"Please," he prompted again, "talk to me, Whitney."

Suddenly suspicious, Whitney withdrew her hands from under
the afghan. "W-why . . . are you here?" she asked, signing rapidly.
"You said you were going back to your apartment . . . to develop
some film."

As if he weren't sure how to answer her, he looked away for an
instant, then returned his searching gaze to her face. "I decided to
drive around for a bit," he told her. "At night, especially, I like to
just—drive around and see what's going on."

At her dubious look, he attempted a smile and added, "I *was* on
my way home. I told you I took rooms just down the street—"

She nodded, and he went on. "I was driving past your house
and saw the lights flashing in back. I thought something might be
wrong, so I stopped."

"How long . . . were you here, before I answered the door?"
Reading his lips, she watched his expression carefully.

"Not long," he replied. "A few minutes, no more. I assumed
you were at home—I saw your car in front—so I was a little
worried when you didn't come to the door right away. Then I
remembered you couldn't hear the bell. I decided to leave and
call the Kaines to let them know about the lights I'd seen, have
them check on you. I was about to go when you came to the
door."

"Did you—" She stopped, then changed her question. "How
many times did you ring the bell?"

He hesitated. "Twice, I believe. But if you can't hear the bell, how did you know—"

"I have a signaling system," she interrupted. The violent trembling had finally stopped, and she was beginning to think a little more clearly. "Certain lights flash . . . in different sequence, depending on whether it's . . . the doorbell or the telephone."

"I see." He paused. "Then the light that was blinking earlier, when I drove by—that was your telephone?"

She nodded and shuddered at the memory. She had been in the bedroom . . . with the doll.

His eyes never left hers. "When you opened the door you were terrified. You still haven't told me why."

Whitney felt an urgency in his gaze, an intensity that somehow made her feel both threatened and protected at the same time.

"Someone . . ." She faltered, swallowed, then tried again. "Someone was . . . here . . . in the house, while I was gone tonight."

As if she had suddenly yanked a string, Devlin's shoulder jerked, his chin lifted, and his eyes went from fire to ice. "What do you mean? How do you know?"

For the first time since she had walked into the bedroom and confronted the horrifying sight on her bed, Whitney felt her fear give way to a swell of anger. "He left a . . . calling card," she said bitterly.

"Where?" His eyes swept the room, then returned to her.

"It's . . . in my bedroom," she said, starting to shrug out from under the afghan.

He leaped to his feet, put a restraining hand on her shoulder. "Stay here. He could still be in the house."

"No," she told him, standing and tossing the afghan onto the couch. "I checked every room, like I always—" She stopped abruptly. Did she really want him to know how much of her life she lived in fear?

He looked at her. "Stay here," he said again. "Which way is the bedroom?"

Whitney pointed to the doorway that led into the breakfast room. "Through there. Across the hall from the kitchen."

After a few minutes, he returned—empty-handed. He stopped in the doorway between the breakfast nook and the living room. "Give me a bag of some sort, would you? A plastic sack will do."

Whitney looked at him blankly.

"For the doll. I want to bag it and the note so I don't lose any fingerprints that might be on them."

He followed her to the kitchen, where she gave him a plastic trash bag.

"Wait here," he said shortly, then turned to leave the room.

Whitney sank down weakly on one of the chairs at the kitchen table and waited.

When he came back, he was carrying the sack, knotted shut. "The police will want this," he said. With an impatient, almost angry motion, he put the sack on the counter by the sink.

"The police?" Whitney stared at him blankly.

He faced her. "Yes. You've called them, haven't you?"

She glanced away. "No, I—I'm not going to call the police."

Frowning, Devlin came to the table where she was sitting, pulled out a chair directly across from her, and straddled it.

Whitney could feel his scrutiny, knew he was waiting for her to meet his eyes.

When she finally looked at him, he searched her face for a moment. "Whitney, Daniel told me about the other night, about what happened to you at the festival. The police need to know about tonight, too. It will affect their investigation of the attack."

Whitney averted her eyes, saying nothing. Only when he reached across the table and touched her hand to get her attention did she meet his gaze.

"Daniel said that the man who attacked you was dressed in the costume of a Pierrot."

Reluctantly, she nodded.

"Does the Pierrot outfit mean anything in particular to you? Is it significant, do you think?"

"What do you mean?" Whitney's hands trembled as she signed the words. She wasn't certain she wanted to know the answer.

"Wasn't Pierrot a character in French pantomime?" he asked, his gaze holding hers.

"I . . . really don't know."

"The *mime,* Whitney," he said, shooting her a look of almost fierce meaning. "That's the connection, wouldn't you think? The mime doesn't speak but simply acts out his desires, his frustrations, from behind a mask of silence."

Devlin hesitated a fraction of a second, then jarred her with a chilling statement. "He knows you, of course."

Whitney tensed.

He went on as if he hadn't noticed. "It would seem to be his idea of a very sick joke, I'd say. By playing the part of a mime, he's actually mocking your deafness."

Unshed tears scalded Whitney's eyes. Her stomach churned in response to his words. *Mocking my deafness . . . Yes, he always did, in one way or another.*

Devlin's arms had been folded on the back of the chair. He freed them now, resting one hand on each side of the high back as he leaned toward her. "Who is he, Whitney?"

She caught her breath. "What?"

"He knows you. He knows you well. And you know him, too. Don't you?"

She shook her head furiously. *"No!"*

His stare remained level. "I see." After a moment, he said, "You don't want to talk about it? There's nothing you want to tell me?"

Again she shook her head, dropping her gaze.

He eased himself off the chair and touched her lightly on the hand until she looked up. "Would you like me to call the police for you?"

"No!" She knew her answer was too quick, too frantic. Groping for a remnant of composure, she finished weakly, "I . . . I don't want the police."

He walked around the table and stood staring down at her, his eyes kind. "Why not, Whitney?"

She could almost feel the gentleness of his tone. He didn't understand, of course. He *couldn't* understand. Anyone else in a similar situation would have called the police long before now.

He lifted a questioning brow. "Whitney?"

She was jolted by the look of compassion in his eyes.

"All right, then," he said. "I'm sure you have your reasons. But what about Jennifer? Shall I call her, ask her to come over?"

Caught off guard by his abrupt acceptance, Whitney rushed to stop him. "N-no, please! I don't want to bring her . . . and Daniel into this. I—it might cause trouble for them."

"But they'd want to help, don't you think?"

When she didn't answer, he pressed. "What about me, then, Whitney? There must be something I can do."

If only there were. Whitney glanced down at the floor, then looked up at him, shaking her head.

When the lights over the sink began to flash, they both jumped. Whitney pushed herself away from the table and got up. "The telephone," she explained.

Crossing the room to a small table beside the window, she lifted the receiver, connected it to her TDD, and keyed in, "Hello." She waited as the answering message appeared on the telecommunications LCD display, indicating the presence of the relay operator.

"Whitney? It's Jennifer. Are you all right? I called earlier to make sure you got home all right, but you didn't answer."

Sensing the concern behind Jennifer's inquiry, Whitney quickly reassured her, glancing at Devlin as she typed.

"I'm fine, Jennifer."

Again, the display responded, "Everything's all right, then?"

Devlin came up and stood behind her, watching over her shoulder.

"Yes. Yes, everything is fine."

"Good. Sleep well. I'll call you tomorrow."

"All right. Good night, Jennifer."

After she had replaced the receiver, Devlin stepped back. "She's very protective of you, isn't she?"

Whitney was immediately defensive. "She's a good friend."

"I wasn't being critical. On the contrary, I find myself liking Jennifer and her remarkable husband very much."

Whitney relaxed. "They've been wonderful to me."

He nodded slowly. "And you're afraid they'll be hurt." His eyes seemed to probe right to the center of her heart. "That's it, isn't it, Whitney? You're afraid that anyone who tries to help you will be hurt."

She backed away from him. "Please, don't . . ."

He lifted a hand, made a short dismissing motion. "It's all right, you don't have to tell me. But at least let me take that—" He glanced over at the plastic sack on the counter. "Let me take it to the police and tell them what's going on."

She shook her head in dismay. "No! I told you . . ."

"Whitney—please"

Even though she couldn't hear Devlin's voice, Whitney sensed the urgency of his words. "You have your reasons for not wanting anyone to know what's going on. But you're taking a very foolish and very dangerous risk."

Whitney started to interrupt, but he ignored her. "I can talk to the police, alert them to the fact that you need protection. I can explain your—your desire for privacy so that they'll respect it. I understand how their minds work. I used to be one of them, you know."

"You don't understand. . . ."

He was obviously losing patience. "I understand," he said, his chin lifting aggressively, "that you have your reasons for not wanting publicity. You made that clear earlier tonight when I suggested getting you some exposure for the Association. And a police investigation—" He shrugged meaningfully. "Well, such an investigation is seldom kept under wraps from the local newspapers."

He stopped, released a long breath, and crossed his arms over his chest. His expression softened again. "You have to trust some-one sometime, Whitney."

She bristled, glaring at him. "I trust my God."

He looked at her for a long tense moment. "I'm sure you do," he finally said, his features now cold and implacable. "I'm simply suggesting that you might want to apply a bit of common sense to your faith."

She flinched at the obvious contempt in his expression. Anger struggled with humiliation until she suddenly remembered some-thing she had seen in his face earlier that evening, when they were leaving the church after the prayer service.

Several members of the congregation had come around to intro-duce themselves to Devlin. As Whitney watched the interchange, she had seen his seemingly ironclad composure begin to slip.

The natural, ebullient friendliness of the small church family had seemed to throw the lean-faced journalist momentarily off balance. Watching him during that unguarded moment, Whitney had been reminded of an ill-at-ease, lonely adolescent, unable to respond to any semblance of warmth or affection. Devlin had actually looked as if he'd like nothing better than to turn and run.

Her irritation with him faded with the memory of that

unguarded look of loneliness she had seen in his eyes. Apparently Devlin had built his own wall of self-defense, just as she had.

Sagging with fatigue and defeat, she said, "Do you really think the police . . . will listen to you? That they'd keep this . . . quiet?"

He blinked. "Yes. I do, Whitney." His eyes willed her to believe him.

Whitney knew he was in no position to offer her that kind of reassurance. But she also told herself that he was at least partially right. She had to use some common sense, take *some* measure of precaution.

She was admitting it was Cory. . . .

Of course, it was Cory! It couldn't be anyone else!

But how? They had told her it would be years before he'd be free . . . if ever.

It didn't matter what they had told her . . . it was *him*. Cory. As insane, as vicious, as dangerous as ever. He was free . . . and he had found her.

"Whitney?"

Numbly, she stared at Devlin, wanting to believe him, needing desperately to trust him.

Finally she whispered, "All right. Yes . . . take it out of here. Please. Just . . . get rid of it."

At the front door, he turned to her. "They connected my phone this morning." Propping the plastic bag by the door for a moment, he pulled a small pad and a pencil from his jacket pocket.

"Here's my number," he told her, scrawling across the top sheet of the pad, then tearing it free and pressing it into her hand. "Memorize it. Your number will show on the caller I.D. I'll know it's you and I'll come right away." He looked at her. "You will call, won't you?"

Whitney hesitated but finally nodded.

"Remember, just call if you need me, and I'll come." He picked up the plastic bag and moved to open the door.

Abruptly he turned back to her, searching her eyes. "That's a promise, Whitney. If you need me, I'll come."

Whitney's throat tightened at the softness, the depth of kindness she encountered in his eyes.

"Tomorrow," he said, reaching for the doorknob, "I'll come by and rig your windows so they can't be so easily opened. That's how he got in, you see. Through that rickety bedroom window in the back. I've got it jammed for now, but I want to do something a bit more permanent to it and the others."

She studied his face intently, her hands signing automatically. "Why are you doing all this . . . for me?"

For a moment he looked as if he would answer. Instead, he simply gave her a small, uncertain smile, lifted his shoulders in a helpless shrug, then turned and opened the door to leave.

The total and immediate chill he left in his wake stunned her. Pressing her face against the cold wood of the door, Whitney squeezed her eyes shut, fighting against the hammering urge to call him back.

Finally, she turned and faced the empty, shadowed living room, forcing herself to accept what had come.

It was upon her again, the lonely, nightmare vigil of terror she had thought forever ended. Now would begin the agonizing struggle for courage, the wrenching prayers for strength, the desperate groping for faith enough to survive the fear.

"The Lord is the stronghold of my life—of whom shall I be afraid?" Her mind latched onto the verse like a lifeline.

But, Father . . . I am afraid. . . . Forgive me, but I'm so terribly afraid.

EIGHT

H
E stood in the deep shadows of the room, glaring angrily into the darkness.

Finally he moved, flinging his coat and cap over a chair. He began to stalk back and forth across the kitchen floor, yanking at his knuckles as he fought down the debilitating rage hovering just beyond the fringes of his mind.

This wasn't how he'd planned it. It was never going to work. She was supposed to be alone. Completely alone.

His entire plan depended on her vulnerability, her solitary life-style. Now it seemed that he was going to have to deal with those two busybodies before he could go any further.

She had always been one to get herself involved in other people's problems. He thought he had cured her of that, but apparently she needed another lesson.

He dropped down on a kitchen chair and, leaning forward, began to massage first one knee, then the other.

All right, so he'd have to back up and rewrite a couple of scenes. No big deal. All he had to do was get rid of the extras.

His frown changed to a smile. That Kaine woman was pretty tight with her new little friend. Always hovering around, like she had to protect the poor little deaf girl. She had to go—and soon.

But first he wanted to deal with the blind man. He nodded to himself. Sure, he'd start with Kaine. He would be the easiest. Then the meddling wife would be no problem.

Abruptly, he hauled himself to his feet. Easing into a set of tension-relieving exercises, he continued to plan.

It just made sense to get Kaine out of the picture first. Even blind, a giant like that one could be trouble. He looked as if he'd have the strength of three men.

But he'd be a pushover for an accident.

After a few minutes he walked over to the window and stared out into the thick, silent darkness, thinking.

What would be the best way to put Kaine out of business? He would have to be careful. A handicapped guy running a radio station in a small burg like this would be well known. Anything suspicious with a blind man, and the cops would be all over it.

No, it couldn't be anything obvious. It had to be an accident. A blind man would naturally be accident-prone, wouldn't he?

But where? He would have to get Kaine alone, without the guide dog. And from what he'd seen, that wouldn't be easy. The dog seemed to go everywhere the blind man went.

A dog like that would be smart, too. Highly trained. He shook his head. It would be considerably easier if he could get Kaine by himself.

Shrugging, he turned away from the window, his eyes roaming over the shadows of the room. He'd work it out. The thing to do was to come up with a plan that had a chance of getting by the dog, just in case he couldn't isolate the blind man.

If that didn't work, he'd go to Plan B.

Feeling good now—loose and confident and powerful—he flexed his shoulder muscles a couple of times and started toward the bedroom.

There was just enough moonlight filtering through the window to let him find the suitcase at the foot of the bed. He

stooped to open it, fumbling through the neatly folded stacks
until he found some clean clothes and his manicure set.

He straightened, running a hand over his face, then passing it
through his hair. He'd wash up and get some sleep. In the morning, he'd be fresher, better able to work out a plan for Kaine.
Something for tomorrow night, hopefully. He didn't want to stay
in one place any longer than he had to. The sooner he sidelined
those yokels running interference for Whitney, the sooner he
could make his move on her, take her out of this hick city.

He nodded decisively, tucking the clothes and the manicure kit
under his arm. Then, pursing his lips in a soft whistle, he turned
and left the room.

NINE

H ADN'T we better get out of here, Daniel? It's almost ten o'clock, and we still have to pick up Jason at your mother's."

Daniel smiled as he heard Jennifer swallow her own words with an enormous yawn. "Come on, boss, give it a rest. This is the second night this week we've worked late. We're going to get another lecture from your dad about stress if we don't watch it."

"As if he's ever put in a normal eight-hour day in his life." Daniel stood up from his desk and stretched his arms above his head. His shoulders felt stiff, and his neck ached. He could use a few laps in the pool.

"But as Lucas would remind you, *he's* a doctor."

"Right. And as we both know—"

"You don't go into medicine if you want a nine-to-five day," they chimed in singsong unison, echoing Lucas Kaine's automatic reply when Daniel's mother scolded him for working too hard.

Daniel touched the face of his Braille watch. "We should have told Mom that Jason could spend the night. Tomorrow is Saturday, after all."

"He just spent last weekend with Gabe and Lyss. The child spends as much time with your family as he does at home."

Picking up a handful of Braille programming charts, Daniel thumped them on the worktable a few times to make a stack. "It's good for him. He had almost eight years in the children's home with no family. Let him enjoy what he's got," he said firmly.

"I suppose you're right," said Jennifer, "You know I'd never tell him so, but Gabe is sorely missed around here. The workload is nearly double without him." She came around the table and took the charts from him. "This is the last batch. I'll put them in my office with the others."

Daniel caught her by the waist. "Suppose you could stop being efficient long enough to hug your husband?"

"I get paid for being efficient."

"But you're on overtime," he told her, taking the charts and returning them to the table. "And since you don't get paid for overtime—"

"Don't I know it!"

"You might as well relax."

She came into his arms with a soft little laugh, smelling like sunshine and warming his heart with love. He leaned down and kissed her, savoring her closeness.

"Mm. My kind of hug," she said, drawing even closer.

Daniel buried his face in her hair. "I love you, darlin'. Or have I already told you that today?"

"You might want to run it by me again in case I missed it the first few times."

He held her close for a moment, then kissed her again.

At her sigh, he lifted an eyebrow. "What's that for?"

She eased back but stayed within the circle of his arms. "Did I tell you about my conversation with Whitney this afternoon?"

"No. But you're going to, right?"

"I am *so* worried about her, Daniel. She seemed very—*strange* on the phone."

"Strange?"

Her answer came without hesitation. "Evasive. She sounded

evasive. And what really upsets me—she's having dinner with Michael Devlin tomorrow night."

Daniel was unable to suppress a smile. "I think that's perfectly acceptable behavior for two single adults, Jennifer."

"She doesn't *know* him, Daniel."

He shrugged. "That's what dating is about, isn't it? Getting to know one another?"

"It's different with Whitney."

"How is it different with Whitney?" he asked patiently.

"Because of what happened to her the other night, Daniel!" she snapped. "For goodness' sake, she was *attacked*. In an alley!"

He nodded slowly. He really did understand her concern. And he knew his wife well enough to know there was no talking her out of it. Actually, to some extent, he shared Jennifer's protective instincts toward Whitney Sharyn. What he didn't share was her distrust of Devlin.

"Look at it this way, Jennifer. Dev might be a good man to have around in case of trouble. You're talking about a guy who's probably been face-to-face with every kind of crisis situation imaginable, even terrorism. Maybe it wouldn't be such a bad thing if he and Whitney were to spend some time together."

"You like him," she said flatly, as if that explained the aberration in his reasoning.

"Let's not start on that," he warned, tightening his hands around her waist.

Again she sighed, and he knew the conversation was a standoff. He brushed a quick kiss across her forehead. "Do what you must with those charts," he said, "and let's get out of here."

He followed her to the door of the office. "How long are you going to be?"

"Just a few minutes. I want to put the charts away and clear off my desk."

"I'm going to get some air." He turned back in the direction of his desk. "Sunny, you can stay. I'll be right back."

The night felt good. For the first time in over a week, the mercury had climbed well above freezing. The station sat at the top of one of the highest hills in the area, so there was always a breeze. Tonight, however, the air was unusually mild.

Daniel stood just outside the door on the small concrete porch, breathing in the scent of wood smoke and spruce. The encircling oaks and sugar maples whispered to each other amid the soft scratching of fallen leaves.

It was his favorite time of the year, always had been. Like the grandfather for whom he had been named, Daniel loved these mountains and had never owned the slightest desire to live anywhere else.

"The Lord made everything beautiful in its own time, Danny-Boy," his grandfather had more than once remarked. "But to my way of thinking, he made these mountains beautiful *all* the time."

An active man until the day he died, his grandfather had had a favorite sport or event for each season. Daniel smiled a little at the undeniable similarity in their natures. Like his grandfather, he liked to be moving. Skiing and ice skating in the winter, climbing or white-water rafting in the summer, horseback riding and hiking in the spring and fall.

His blindness had slowed him down some, but mostly he still did what he wanted to do. Skiing was the exception. There was something about racing down a mountain into the vast unknown that he couldn't quite handle.

A thought struck him as he walked across the porch.

Wouldn't Grandpa Dan have taken a shine to Jennifer? The old man's stubbornness and Jennifer's feistiness would have been something to behold. The two of them would have scrapped from sunup to sundown, with his grandfather loving every fiery minute of it. And loving Jennifer at the same time. Oh yes, he surely would have loved her.

She's an easy woman to love, my wife. . . .

That honey-voiced rebel had captured his heart the first day she crashed into his life. He shoved his hands into his pockets and lifted his face, letting the night air wash over him. *If only she weren't such a mother hen . . .*

Not that she'd ever change. He supposed Jennifer's propensity for caregiving had been shaped years ago. When her mother died, she had cared for two younger brothers. Her father, a high school band director, had taken on private students during evenings and weekends to help pay the outrageous medical bills left over from his wife's illness. Although Jennifer would never have admitted it—probably hadn't even realized it—she had sacrificed a great deal in her determination to take as much pressure as she possibly could off her father's shoulders.

That kind of responsibility thrust upon a sixteen-year-old girl, in combination with her natural protective instincts, had most likely set the course for Jennifer's life. She was fiercely defensive of those she cared for . . . and couldn't seem to help trying to manage their lives.

And he loved her for it. *Oh, dear Lord, how I love her. . . . I'll praise you and thank you every day of my life for giving me this woman to love.*

Smiling, Daniel freed one hand, felt for the wrought-iron railing by the steps, and started down.

A sharp, stunned cry of alarm exploded from him as his left foot caught and pitched him forward. He grabbed for the railing, finding nothing but air.

He groped desperately for the touch of wrought iron on either side, but it was too late. He shot out over the steps, crashing onto the concrete walk at the bottom. His left leg buckled under him, snapping so fast and hard he roared in agony.

The pain seized him, sending shock waves raging through his entire body. He shouted again, but the sound was cut short by a sudden onslaught of weakness.

He tried to raise himself off his leg but fell forward with the effort. Fighting against the nausea that welled up in his throat, he called Jennifer's name with as much strength as he could muster, knowing even as he cried out how unlikely it was that she would hear him.

At the door to her office, Jennifer put a hand to the light switch, paused, then turned to glance back at the charts now neatly stacked on the worktable near the desk. After an instant she sighed with weary satisfaction, turned off the overhead light, and closed the door.

Crossing the hall toward Daniel's office, she heard Sunny bark once, then again, louder.

"Yes, I know, girl," she said conversationally. "He forgot about us again. Most likely he's out there hugging a tree or talking to the moon or whatever the man does when he disappears after dark. Why don't we just go ahead and lock up? Then we'll track him down."

But when she entered the office, there was no sign of the retriever. Puzzled, she went to look behind the desk. It wasn't like Sunny to disobey Daniel. When the retriever was told to stay, she stayed. Always.

Jennifer whirled around in surprise at the sound of Sunny's furious barking. She stared blankly at the open door for an instant, then finally moved, bolting from the office and half running down the hall.

She stopped short when she reached the receptionist's desk, bewildered by the sight of an obviously agitated Sunny. The dog was prancing back and forth in front of the double entrance doors, no longer barking but whining with apparent frustration.

As soon as the retriever saw Jennifer, she bounded toward her, her desperate barking renewed.

Jennifer put a hand on the dog's head to try to soothe her. "It's all right, girl. Settle down."

But Sunny wouldn't settle. Instead, she turned in the direction of the door, then back to Jennifer.

"Sunny? What is it, girl? What do you want?"

The dog dashed to the door, turned to Jennifer and barked savagely.

Something was wrong. Sunny wouldn't carry on this way for no reason. Even when she was impatient to go outside, her demeanor was calm as she waited for someone to take notice.

But now, as if to rebuke Jennifer for her delay, the dog turned frenzied dark eyes in her direction and continued to bark. In that instant, it dawned on Jennifer that the object of the retriever's agitation was outside.

Her heart began to hammer. *"Daniel!"*

Jennifer charged for the double door, flinging both sides open with a force that sent them banging against the wall. The retriever slipped by her like a golden streak and bolted across the porch.

Jennifer followed, catching her breath at the sight of Daniel lying prostrate on the concrete walk, bent and huddled in obvious agony.

TEN

L UCAS Kaine crossed his arms over his chest and
surveyed his efforts with a clinical eye. The
completed cast covered a little over half of Daniel's
left leg.

"I'm going to admit you for the rest of the night," he said. As if
anticipating a challenge from his son, he added, "It's almost two
now. I want your circulation monitored for the next few hours.
We'll get you released before noon if everything looks all right."

With a distracted glance down the splattered front of his blue
scrub suit, he headed for the sink in the corner of the room to
clean up.

Now that she could finally move in closer to Daniel, Jennifer
clung to his hand, closely studying his face for any lingering signs
of pain. His complexion wasn't quite as pasty as it had been when
the medics had first brought him in on the cart. Still, she felt a
pang of concern at the drawn, haggard set of his features.

"How long, Dad?" Daniel's voice was quiet but edged with
strain. "How long will I have to wear this—thing?"

Lucas slowly turned around, wiping his hands on a white hospital towel. As he came to stand at the foot of the examining table,
Jennifer was struck again by the marked resemblance between
Daniel and his father. A big man, Lucas Kaine's size was still less
formidable than that of his son. Both men, however, had the same

incredibly deep blue eyes, the same high, prominent cheekbones, and the same rather arrogant, hawkish nose that Daniel's sister often referred to as "the mark of Kaine."

Lucas smoothed his thick silver hair with one hand as he quietly studied his son's face. With obvious reluctance, he finally answered. "Too long to suit you, I expect. It'll be a few weeks before we can put you in a walking cast."

"A few *weeks?*" With a stunned, incredulous expression, Daniel pushed himself up on his elbows. "I'm going to be laid up for *weeks?* Come on, Dad—I broke my *leg,* not my back!"

"Daniel," Lucas said, glancing at Jennifer as he spoke, "you're the one who insisted on a cast instead of surgery. That doesn't change the fact that you've broken your leg—your shinbone, to be exact, as well as fracturing a couple of other bones. This is going to take time." He paused. "And it is also going to take your full cooperation."

With a groan that squeezed Jennifer's heart, Daniel fell back onto the examining table.

Jennifer exchanged a look with Lucas. She felt certain they were both concerned about the same thing. This unexpected curtailment of activity would increase the burden of Daniel's blindness.

Her throat tightened, and she glanced away. For a moment, her gaze roamed the aging examining room with its faded white paint and outdated fixtures. It was, she decided, a drab, depressing room.

She turned back to Daniel, determined to sound more cheerful than she felt. "It won't be so bad," she said, her words spilling out in a rush as she bent over him. "You'll probably be able to go back to work in a few days." She shot a questioning glance at her father-in-law.

When Lucas merely lifted his brows and inclined his head in an expression of uncertainty, Jennifer scrambled for some scrap of reassurance to offer her husband. "What we have to do, Daniel, is just—keep busy. And there are lots of things you can do at home. You can work on the ensemble music for the teens . . . and you have some new books on tape you haven't had time to listen to yet. And, Daniel, this would be a perfect time to start getting some notes together for that workshop we're going to be doing next spring in Kentucky, the one Mitch wrote to you about."

He didn't answer.

As if to give Jennifer's efforts a boost, Lucas interjected a hopeful note of his own. "You'll be able to get around on crutches in a few days, son. This is going to slow you down a little, true, but it's not as if you'll be totally immobile."

Jennifer gave her father-in-law a grateful smile and squeezed Daniel's hand. "Cheer up, darling. Please."

He turned his face toward her and finally, with obvious effort, managed a smile and a small nod. "I'm OK. Just tired."

"You need to rest," Lucas agreed, "but Rick Hill is still out in the waiting room. I promised you'd see him after we got the cast on."

"Who called the police?" Daniel asked with no real show of interest.

"The ward secretary," his father replied. "Mary Ryan called me out of CCU to talk with Jennifer when she called, and I asked her to call the squad and the police while I changed into my scrubs."

"We were talking just tonight about your long hours, Lucas," Jennifer told him. "For once I'm glad you *weren't* at home."

"Pauline says I never am." He grinned at Jennifer. "Listen, I'm going to change before this plaster sets up and I have to wear these scrubs forever. Is it all right if Rick comes in now?"

Daniel nodded. "I can't tell him much, but send him in."

Lucas started toward the door, then turned back to Jennifer. "Where's Jason? Is he still at our house?"

"Yes. We were just getting ready to leave the station and come after him—"

He nodded, making it unnecessary for her to finish. "I suppose you intend to spend the rest of the night here, too?"

"Yes," Jennifer said, giving Daniel no chance to object. "When I called Pauline, she said she had already put Jason to bed."

"All right. I'll look in before I leave for home." Lucas glanced once more at Jennifer, then Daniel. "They'll get you settled in a private room as soon as you've talked with Rick. And I'll leave instructions for pain medication over the next few hours. Just tell one of the nurses when you need it."

The uniformed patrolman who entered the examining room after Lucas left was young, fair-haired, and, Jennifer knew, from previous experience, extremely capable.

Holding his cap under one arm, he greeted them and then went to stand beside Daniel at the examining table.

"Dan. Sorry about this. Can you tell me anything that will help?"

Daniel smiled grimly and shook his head. "Dad said you've already been up to the station?"

The officer nodded. "Right. I wanted to see that piece of wire across the step before it was taken down."

He glanced at Jennifer. "You were inside the station when it happened, weren't you, Mrs. Kaine?"

"Yes. Daniel had gone out on the porch to get some air," Jennifer explained. "I was just getting ready to lock up when Sunny started barking in the lobby."

"You left Sunny inside, Dan?" The officer glanced across the examining table to the retriever sitting alertly at Daniel's side. Her ears pricked up at the sound of her name.

Daniel nodded. "I hadn't planned to stay outside more than a couple of minutes."

"Did you hear anything at all before this happened?" the patrolman asked, frowning as he studied the cumbersome cast on Daniel's leg.

"Nothing but the wind. Someone could have been out there, I suppose, but I didn't hear anything."

"Rick—"

The officer looked at Jennifer, waiting.

"I don't think anyone was around. Sunny would have sensed it, and she never budged from Daniel's side once we got outside."

Nodding at Jennifer's logic, the patrolman wrote something in his notebook. "Nothing unusual happened around the station today? No peculiar phone calls or anything like that?"

Again, Daniel shook his head. "Not that I'm aware of."

Jennifer agreed. "Nothing."

The officer tucked the notebook back into his pocket. "Well—it's not much, but we'll do what we can."

"What kind of wire was it, do you know?" Daniel asked.

"Not yet. It's thin, flexible—it looks to me like the stuff my wife uses in the craft shop, but I'm not sure." He paused. "It's thin enough that it would be hard to see, especially at night. I'm not so sure even your dog would have spotted it, Dan."

His expression glum, Daniel shook his head with conviction. "Sunny would have spotted it. I wouldn't be in this mess if I had taken her with me."

The officer's look was sympathetic. "Well, I'll get back to you as soon as I know anything."

He stepped away from the table, then turned back. "Dan, what's your feeling about this? Any idea who might be responsible?"

Daniel frowned. "No. It doesn't make any sense to me."

"Mrs. Kaine?"

Jennifer shook her head in frustration. "I can't imagine who—or *why*," she replied, her voice trembling. "Only a sick mind would do something like this."

The officer nodded. "Well, if you happen to think of anything that might be important, just give us a call. Dan—take care. I'll be in touch." He stopped. "How's Miss Sharyn doing, by the way?" he asked Jennifer. "No more trouble since the night of the festival, I hope?"

"No, she's just fine," Jennifer answered with a smile. "I'll tell her you asked about her."

With another small nod, the policeman left the room.

Jennifer bent over and brushed a light kiss across Daniel's forehead. "Are you feeling terrible?"

His smile failed. "Probably not the way you mean."

Jennifer frowned.

He let out a long breath. "This is going to be a real bummer, Jennifer. For both of us."

"Daniel—"

He waved off her attempt to console him. "Why don't you see if they have a room ready for me yet, would you? I'm beat."

Jennifer studied him, wishing that Lucas hadn't left.

"Jennifer?"

"Yes, all right, I'll go check. Would you like me to see about some pain medication, too, Daniel? I think you ought to have—"

"Just a bed," he said shortly. "And, Jennifer—*please* don't . . . hover. I don't need a private nurse. I just need some sleep."

Stung by his sharpness, Jennifer blinked back tears as she moved away from the examining table.

He didn't mean it, she told herself all the way out the door and down the hall. He was in pain, he was exhausted, and he had been through a terrible experience. Who *wouldn't* be impatient and cross?

Spying Lucas at the nurse's station at the far end of the hall, she gave a sigh of relief and began to walk a little faster.

She was simply going to have to be patient with Daniel. He'd be fine in a few days; she'd see to it. She mustn't hover, though.

She knew how much Daniel hated that kind of thing. It had been one of his biggest frustrations in the months following the accident that had blinded him. The attempts of his family and friends to protect him had made it almost impossible for him to have any privacy, he had told her. Everyone had made such a business of protecting him that they had very nearly *suffocated* him.

Well, I am not *going to make the same mistake,* she told herself, even though he was clearly expecting her to "hover." She would surprise him.

She *would.*

ELEVEN

D EVLIN pulled in at the curb, put the Bronco in park, and let the motor idle. Turning the heater fan to low, he cut the headlights and switched on the parking and interior lights. The windshield wipers continued to thump, spreading the driving rain into scattered sheets across the glass.

"Nice night," he said with a cynical lift of one eyebrow.

Whitney smiled at his expression, then glanced out the front windshield. She could see nothing except a distorted splash of asphalt.

"I like the rain," she confessed. "When I was little, I used to . . . sneak outside at night and just sit on the porch and watch the rain." She turned back to him. "Does it rain a lot . . . in Ireland? You know . . . the 'emerald hills' . . . and the 'shamrock fields'?"

He was leaning back, an arm draped comfortably across the top of the seat, his face turned toward her. There was the faintest hint of a smile in his eyes, and his features gentled even more as he studied her face. Suddenly, he laughed, and Whitney was once again jolted by the unexpected transformation. Without the grim, hard set to his mouth and the brooding darkness in his eyes, he looked years younger.

"I wouldn't want to shatter your image of the land, but I'm afraid it's not as green and golden as you may have read." He looked away for a moment, and when he turned back to her, his expression had changed. "For years now, our hills and fields have run red."

So strong was the bitter sorrow in his expression that Whitney felt as if he had touched her. "Is that why you left?" she asked hesitantly. "Because of the violence?"

His eyes turned bleak as he looked, not at her, but into the darkness beyond the window on her side. "In a way, yes." For a moment he seemed to stare at something in the distance. Then he blinked, regarding her as if suddenly remembering her presence.

Pain. Whitney could see it in him. A terrible pain, eating at him, chipping away at him.

"Do you think . . . you'll ever go back?" she asked.

Whitney thought she had seen pain before, but now she instinctively drew away from the raw anguish glistening in Michael Devlin's eyes. The hand resting on the steering wheel tightened, clenching the rim in a white-knuckled grasp. For one irrational moment, Whitney wanted to touch him, comfort him. She tightened her own hand into a fist to curb the impulse.

"It's hard to say," Devlin finally answered, shaking his head as he spoke. "I don't think so. I'm an American citizen now."

"A citizen? I didn't realize . . . you had been here that long. But wouldn't you want to go back for a visit someday?"

He looked at her and shrugged. "I've no one to visit."

Whitney found it unsettling to realize how little she knew about this man—and how much she wanted to know. He continued to slip in and out of her days, puzzling her with his questions, his apparent interest in her, and his multifaceted personality that seemed to have no end to its contrasts and contradictions.

Just as he had promised, he had shown up on Thursday to secure her windows with a simple crossed-nail gimmick. He had grumbled and groused most of the time he was there about the locks on the front office door and the one on the connecting door to her apartment, demanding a promise from her that she would have both replaced as soon as possible. Then, in almost the same breath, he had flashed that short-circuiting smile of his and asked her to dinner on Friday.

It could have been an evening to turn her head if Devlin had behaved more like an interested suitor and less like a journalist. Not, she had hastily reminded herself, that she was ready to think of any man as a "suitor." Certainly not now . . . perhaps not ever.

Still, tonight had been permeated with a heady, romantic atmosphere—a small, private dining room with candlelight and, Devlin had informed her, "weeping violins" in the background.

Sitting across the table from the enigmatic Irishman, watching the candlelight shadows play over his face as he concentrated his attention on her, it would have been all too easy to forget her determination to keep things impersonal.

Devlin, however, had made it entirely possible for her to maintain a safe emotional distance. For over two hours, Whitney felt as if she were being *interviewed,* not courted—interviewed by a smooth professional with the formidable combination of a journalist's technique and a policeman's authority.

Frequently during the evening, she had felt tense and on edge, trying to stay one step ahead of his skillful, sharply arrowed questions.

At one point, irritated and unsettled by queries that bordered on invasiveness, Whitney had virtually snapped at him. "Are you writing a book, Mr. Devlin?"

He blinked and grinned, apparently unruffled by her peevishness. "Michael," he corrected automatically. Without missing a beat, he immediately skated into another question about her background.

Her exasperation with him had ebbed once he apologized. "I'm afraid I forget how wholly obnoxious an ex-cop turned journalist can be to a normal person like yourself. I suppose I've been acting like a wolfhound worrying a bone."

"As a matter of fact," Whitney told him with exaggerated sweetness, "you have."

"Old habits die hard, you see," he said with an apologetic smile.

Whitney was fairly certain that she had told him no more than she wanted him to know. Certainly, she knew little more about *him* than she had at the beginning of the evening.

Now she decided to try to focus the conversation on him. "Tell me about Belfast," she said. "I'm afraid the only thing . . . I know about it is that—" She paused, concentrating to make sure her *t*s didn't come out sounding like *d*s. "That the *Titanic* was built there."

He nodded. "There's not much else worth knowing."

"You don't sound very . . . fond . . . of your home."

He looked at her, his expression taking on the familiar fixed mask. "It's difficult to be fond of Belfast. She's a sour old city: somber, rather dismal, and not especially hospitable. It has something to do with bombs being tossed back and forth in the streets and children being murdered in their schoolyards, I suspect."

His jawline looked as if it were cut from stone.

"It must have been . . . difficult to be a policeman in a situation like that," Whitney ventured.

His eyes turned bitter. "You can't be a policeman in Belfast. You can be a warrior or a terrorist or a soldier or a killer. But you can't possibly be a policeman." He stopped. His next words came slowly, as if directed to himself. "A police officer is meant to be a keeper of the peace, you see. But in Belfast there has never been any peace to keep. The entire city has been a battleground for years, and peace is spoken of only at funerals."

In a clear attempt to change the subject, he transferred his gaze to her house, almost totally obscured by the night and the curtain of rain washing down the window on her side. "This is a wonder-

ful neighborhood, you know. I'll most likely use a shameful
amount of film on it. It's a remarkable town, isn't it? Few things fit
the word *quaint* any longer, but Shepherd Valley seems to wear the
word well."

Whitney nodded in agreement, once more feeling her balance
tilt as she watched his dour mood change to an almost boyish
enthusiasm. "I love it here. I hope . . . I never have to leave."

His gaze roamed her face, his mouth softening to a smile. "Yes,
I would imagine you to be one for home and hearth fire, Whitney Sharyn."

Whitney suddenly found herself wishing she could hear his
voice, listen to him say her name. She thought his words would
glide and flow with rhythm. Somehow she knew his voice would
be melodic, low-pitched with an easy lilt. He smiled again, his
eyes twinkling with a look of affection so warm she lost her
breath at it.

When the moment became awkward, Devlin stirred, dropping
his arm from the back of the seat. "I suppose we should be getting you inside. The rain's eased a bit."

He turned off the lights and pulled his keys from the ignition,
then opened the door on his side and got out.

The earlier downpour had diminished to a steady, but lighter,
rain. They bolted up the steps and through the gate, then took off
running down the walk until, laughing, they reached the back
porch.

Whitney watched him fit the key into the lock. His rain-
soaked hair had begun to curl at the ends, and his eyes were still
dancing with laughter. Pushing the door open with one hand, he
watched her until she brushed by him and went inside.

In the landing, Whitney turned, expecting to say good night.
Instead, Michael stepped inside, clearly feeling no need for an invitation.

"I'll have a look through the house before I leave," he said, wiping his feet on the floor mat.

"No . . . I mean, that's not necessary."

"I'd feel better," he replied, his glance going from her face to the wall switch at his side. He reached for it, flipped it on.

She frowned up at him. "Michael . . . I can't have someone . . . following me into the house every time I . . . come home after dark."

"You can if I'm the one who brings you home," he replied with a deceptively bland look.

"But—"

"You'd best get out of that raincoat." He turned and headed for the living room.

Instead, Whitney followed him to the doorway, waiting until he turned on the table lamp.

She started into the room, but he lifted a hand, indicating that she should wait for him.

Whitney returned to the entrance hall, set her purse on the desk, then hung up her raincoat. As she shook off the dampness, she remembered that she hadn't talked with Jennifer yet today. She had tried the house several times throughout the afternoon with no response. They didn't talk every day, but most Saturdays they had a lengthy phone conversation to catch up.

She glanced at her watch. Almost ten o'clock. Even if Michael were to leave within the next few minutes, she couldn't call Jennifer this late. They'd have to talk at church in the morning.

On her way back into the living room, she stopped at the thermostat to turn up the furnace.

After a few minutes, Michael returned. "All seems normal," he announced. "Where's the key for the office? I'll have a look in there as well."

"Oh, really, that's not—"

"It won't take but a moment," he interrupted. "The key?"

Whitney retrieved the key from her purse in the hall and slapped it into the palm of his hand—a little too firmly.

His gaze skimmed her face, and Whitney thought she saw a glint of amusement. Then he winked at her and started down the hallway to the office.

This time, Whitney went with him. When she started through the door ahead of him, he clasped both her shoulders and set her gently but firmly behind him.

The office was cold but appeared to be in order. Michael gave the room an efficient, sharp-eyed sweep, his gaze coming to rest on a small milk-glass lamp on the credenza behind Whitney's desk.

"Do you use that lamp?" he asked abruptly, looking down at her.

"Use it?"

"Could we move it?"

"Move it where?"

"There," he said, inclining his head toward the large front window. "Let's put the lamp in the window. Put a dim bulb in it, and let it burn at night. It would ease my mind a bit. Makes the place look more inhabited."

Whitney shrugged.

"You don't mind? Good." He crossed the room, took the lamp to the window, setting it squarely in the middle of the sill. Plugging the cord into the outlet below the window, he straightened and turned on the switch. "It's a bit bright, but it will do for now. You can change the bulb tomorrow."

He scanned the office once more, then, apparently satisfied, locked the door behind them. As they left the room, he took Whitney by the elbow and crossed the hall to the landing, stopping when they reached the outside door.

"I talked with the police," he said bluntly, still holding her by the arm.

"You did *what?*" She pulled away from him.

He gave a small nod. "Yes. This afternoon. I turned over the doll to them, and I pressed them for additional protection for you because of the break-in. They're aware that you're being harassed and that you think you're being watched." He stopped, studying her face as if to judge her reaction before going on. "There'll be someone by tomorrow to talk with you, to get some more information."

"I *told* you—" Whitney's hands jerked as she signed the words.

He interrupted her with a shake of his head. "Anything you tell them will be held in absolute confidence," he reassured her. "I explained your desire to avoid publicity, and they've agreed to it." He paused, then added, "Whitney, you're going to have to tell them more than you've told me, you know. They can't help you if you don't tell them the truth. All of it."

"It will only . . . make things worse!"

He grasped her by the shoulders almost roughly, his eyes burning into hers. "Whitney—it's time to ask for help, can't you see that? You don't trust me; you don't trust the police— you won't even bring Daniel and Jennifer into your confidence for fear they'll be hurt!"

Stunned by his outburst, Whitney went rigid under his hands.

His gaze suddenly cleared, and he dropped his hands away. "I'm sorry," he said, still searching her eyes. "But you have to protect yourself, Whitney. You spend your life taking care of everyone else, but you won't seek help for yourself. Why?"

He was watching her with obvious concern and perhaps a measure of frustration. Again Whitney had the sensation that this man knew her almost as well as she knew herself—knew her, and *cared* about her. She found the thought both intriguing and unsettling.

She didn't know how to answer him. She stood, staring down at the floor to avoid his probing gaze.

After a moment, he tilted her face upward, holding her gaze with his. "You think I don't understand. But I do, Whitney. I know what you're doing. You're putting yourself in the path of this lunatic because you don't want anyone else to be hurt. This has happened to you before, hasn't it? And now it's happening again."

When she tried to turn away, he cupped her chin, forcing her to look at him. "That's it, isn't it, Whitney?"

Whitney remained stubbornly silent, and he nodded slowly, knowingly. "You're going to say nothing. You're going to watch for a chance, and then you're going to run."

He frowned down at her, his expression urgent. "Whitney, you can't outrun this madman. He'll find you. Wherever you go, he'll find you. You've got to stay and fight, don't you see? Get some help and fight him. For once, you're going to have to take instead of give. Ask for help, Whitney. Please." He paused, brushed her cheek with his fingertips, and said, "Ask me."

Whitney bit her lip to hold back the tears welling in her eyes.

"Who are you?" she whispered fiercely.

"What?" His eyes narrowed.

"Who *are* you?" she repeated, her hands moving rapidly. "You come crashing into my life . . . *demanding* that I do what *you* say . . . as if you have a right! I want to know . . . just who you are!"

The question hung between them in the silence. Finally, with a strange, weary look of resignation, Devlin handed her the office key. "I'm your shadow, Whitney," he said. "From now on, until this is over, I'm going to be your shadow."

He gave her no chance to reply. Instead he turned, opened the door, and walked out into the rainy night.

Whitney closed the door, locked it, and dropped the office key into her purse on the desk. She squeezed her eyes shut, groping for the strength to withstand her warring emotions.

"I'm going to be your shadow. . . ."

Slowly it dawned on Whitney that she had been so intent on keeping Daniel and Jennifer at arm's length . . . for their own protection . . . that she hadn't even considered the threat to Michael Devlin. Somehow, before she had realized what was happening, he had slipped into her life, becoming a part of it, even . . . *important* to it. With a sick sense of despair, she realized that the circle of people who could be hurt because of *her* had grown. Jennifer and Daniel. Even Jason, their son. And now Michael.

She pushed away from the door, walked to the desk, and stood staring down at it, seeing nothing. Her hands gripped the back of the chair. Why had she deluded herself into thinking she had a *choice?* Michael had only been baiting her about running away, of course, but that was just what she would have to do. She couldn't possibly stay here.

Yet how could she ever bring herself to leave? She loved this place—the town, her job, the people—she loved it all. Did she really have to give up everything again?

And how long could she run? Where could she go that he wouldn't find her . . . again?

She shook her head, trying to think. The first thing she needed to do was to find out exactly what had happened, how he had gotten out, how long he had *been* out.

Reaching across the chair, she turned off the desk lamp, then started for the bedroom. If only her parents were back from Florida, she could call them, and perhaps they could contact the state hospital, make an inquiry. But they wouldn't be back in Louisville for several days yet.

She entered the dark bedroom cautiously. Making her way to the night table, she wondered if she would ever again be able to enter this room without remembering that horrible doll.

Whitney turned on the lamp, drawing in a shaky breath of relief when she saw the empty bed. Suddenly the light began to flash the signal for an incoming call.

Shakily she went to the kitchen, connected the TDD, then waited.

It was Jennifer.

Devastated, Whitney watched the message about Daniel's . . . *accident* . . . float across the display. With trembling fingers she responded to Jennifer's news, thankful that her friend couldn't know the panic and fury boiling up in her.

When she finally replaced the receiver, she stood motionless, staring down at the telephone. So she had been right. And now it was beginning.

With wooden steps, she went back to the bedroom and flung herself across the bed. She lay without moving, sick at heart and numb with despair.

He was out. Cory. He was *here*. And Daniel had become his first victim.

TWELVE

THE room was cold and totally dark. Whitney rubbed her eyes, swollen from her bout of weeping and heavy with the beginning of a headache.

She peered into the blackness, an icy dread slowly settling over her. Something was wrong.

She lay unmoving, trying to focus her eyes on some point of reference in the room. She turned her head toward the digital clock on the bedside table. There was no display.

The power was off.

Was that what had awakened her? Had she realized, even while she slept, that the house had been plunged into a frigid darkness?

She turned in the direction of the window across the room. Not a glimmer of light filtered through.

She swung her feet over the bed and got up. The jacket of her dress was crumpled around her waist. She smoothed it; then, shivering from the cold and from a growing sense of apprehension, she fumbled for the brass knob at the foot of the bedstead. Gripping the knob to steady herself, she pulled in a deep breath, then pushed away from the bed and began to edge her way toward the window.

Her feet left the braided rug and met the hardwood floor. She took a few more steps, then stopped short as she stubbed her toe on the rocking chair in front of the window. Swallowing a cry of pain, she skimmed her fingers over the arm of the chair, then pulled the drape aside just enough to allow a narrow view out the window.

For a moment she felt as if she had opened a curtain on the veil of night itself. A dense blackness seemed to have swallowed the entire street. No streetlights relieved the darkness. No stars dotted the sky. Only the black shadows of overhanging trees, their branches writhing in the wind, gave substance and form to the dark canvas.

Her hand clutched the drape, then let it slide through her fingers as she turned back to face the inky depths of the bedroom.

Now she was not only deaf, but for all practical purposes, blind as well.

This is what Daniel Kaine's world is like, she suddenly realized. Dark and shapeless, with the continual threat of the unknown.

The threat. What had Cory said in his note? *"Wait for me, Whitney. I'll be back."*

The stupor of sleep fled as panic seized her. Cory did not make idle threats. Her senses sharpened by fear, she felt as if something had taken hold of her, something cold and deadly and evil. Instinctively, Whitney struck out with both hands, slicing the air in front of her with a wild, frenzied thrashing.

Abruptly, she stopped. *He had come for her. . . . he was in the room, waiting for her to make a move. . . .*

She edged sideways, away from the window, pressing her back to the cold wall. Her mouth was dry, filled with the metallic taste of terror.

No, he wasn't in the room. He would have fallen upon her by now.

But he could easily be somewhere in the house.

Her heart raced. A flashlight. Where had she put her flashlight? She had two: one in the office and another in the kitchen. Where in the kitchen? Where had she last seen it?

The cabinet under the sink.

She felt a sudden, irrational longing for light. Another moment in this darkness would surely take her sanity.

But what if he *was* in the room, waiting?

After another moment of indecision, she squatted down, then went to her hands and knees and began to crawl through the clammy darkness.

The floor was hard and cold beneath her hands. Panic gnawed at the back of her mind. Her stomach pitched with the first throes of nausea.

She went on, feeling her way along the baseboard, desperately praying that she couldn't be seen or heard. She felt like a cornered animal groping its way to freedom.

Cover me with your power, Lord. . . . be my shield, my protector. . . .

She was at the door to the hall. She scrambled through on her knees, paused to catch a breath, then got to her feet.

The hallway was as black as the bedroom. Whitney held her breath and began to move again, skimming along the wall, both hands extended. Chilled, she trembled head to foot, expecting at any moment to be struck or grabbed.

She reached the kitchen, gasped for air, and waited. When nothing happened, she inched forward, around the table, over to the sink.

With one hand braced on the countertop, she grasped the door beneath the sink. It came only partway open, shuddering on its hinge.

Whitney dropped to the floor, trying to force the door, terrified of making a noise that would give her away. Finally the door shot open, almost knocking her off balance.

Heart pounding, she began to fumble among the cleanser and detergent bottles under the sink, trying to be careful. Her hands were shaking uncontrollably as she swept the right side, then the left.

No flashlight.

With the back of one hand, she wiped away tears of frustration, trying to decide what to do next.

For a moment she was overcome by the sensation that somewhere . . . in this room or in another part of the house . . . someone was waiting for her to make an end of her futile attempt to save herself. Then he would pounce on her.

Cory.

Her nerve failed her, but only for a moment. She gasped, trying to pull in more air, swallowing too much and growing dizzy.

She had to get control of herself, had to think. She framed her face with her hands, which by now were ice-cold and damp.

Her head came up as she remembered the knife drawer. She forced herself to slow her breathing, then got to her feet and opened the drawer to her right.

She withdrew a knife, but it was too small.

Fumbling, she pulled out the butcher knife. At the same time, she remembered that both flashlights were in the office.

She had gone upstairs one day last week to get a box of envelopes out of the storage room. Unable to find the office flashlight—and unwilling to chance an encounter with a mouse among the dark corners and dusty cartons stored in the unused rooms—she had taken the flashlight from the kitchen. Later she had found the other flashlight but had left both in her office.

She nearly wept with frustration. The office was at the other end of the house.

And it was locked.

She would need the key from her purse.

And her purse was still on the desk in the entrance hall.

She dragged in a long, shaky breath, trying to think.

All right. She would go through the breakfast nook, back through the living room to the entry. Get the key; go back to the office. Maybe by then the lights would be on.

She got to her feet, using the countertop to steady herself. Then she started to move, making her way out of the kitchen.

The breakfast nook seemed enormous as Whitney moved through it. She swallowed once, then again, against the knot of fear wedged in her throat. Reaching the archway into the living room, she stopped.

Candles.

Of course! There was a candle in almost every room of the house.

And matches. On the mantle above the fireplace.

She started into the living room, turned too sharply and jabbed her elbow against the wall. She stopped, glancing around into the darkness for some sign of movement, then went on. At the fireplace, she slid her hand along the smooth surface of the mantle from one end to the other.

The matches were gone.

Frantic, she started at the other side and tried again, then dropped to her knees and raked the hand without the knife along the hearth.

No matches.

For a moment she stayed on her knees, one hand splayed out in front of her, the other clutching the knife.

It would be so easy to just give up. . . .

She lifted her head. No, she *wouldn't* give up. She hauled herself to her feet and began to follow the wall, shivering at the touch of the cold plaster. For the house to be this cold, the furnace must have been off for hours.

The power *could* be out because of the storm, she told herself. The power might be out all over town, for all she knew.

She edged around the corner into the entrance hall, feeling for the desk. Her hand hit the side of the lamp, and she grabbed at it to keep it from toppling.

She skimmed the desktop with her free hand.

Her purse wasn't there.

She dropped to the floor, thinking she might have knocked it off when she hit the lamp.

The purse wasn't on the floor either.

Whitney scrambled to her feet, her mind racing. Without her purse, she had no keys, couldn't get inside the office, couldn't get the flashlight.

She was trapped in the dark.

Call Michael. . . .

He had told her to call if she needed him, hadn't he? He had given her his number, told her to memorize it—

But she *hadn't*. She had stuffed it down in her purse, looking at it once or twice since without committing it to memory, knowing she wouldn't call him.

She could leave, get out of the house.

No . . . that might be just what he was waiting for. Cory might be waiting outside, waiting until she ran out into the darkness. . . .

Whitney forced herself to think back, to remember how his mind worked. What would he expect her to do?

He would be waiting for her to run. She was certain of it. He had always loved to terrorize her, to wait for her in out-of-the-way places and then jump out at her when she least expected it. He would play his sick practical jokes—cruel stunts that grew more and more sadistic with time—just to make her react. To frighten her. Sometimes he would still be wearing his makeup from the players group, and he would practically throw himself in her way, making those awful faces, laughing at her when she panicked.

Her only hope was to hide from him, to find a safe place and stay put until the lights came back on—or until daylight, if necessary.

But if he was inside the house, there *was* no safe place.

A fresh wave of panic squeezed her throat. Her breathing came in a rush. Her heart pounded so hard it felt as if each beat might

break through her chest. Somehow she willed herself to inch down the wall, toward the hall closet. Propelled by fear, she opened the closet door and stood staring into a darkness as thick as that of the rest of the house.

Expelling a long, tremulous breath, she wedged herself into the closet, pulling the door shut behind her, squeezing back behind the out-of-season clothing she kept stored there. She sank down in the corner, pressing herself as tightly as possible against the wall.

Chilled, she huddled there, hugging her knees, clutching the knife, struggling for control.

She had hidden from him before. Many times. It felt almost natural to be skulking in a corner again, waiting for him to find her, praying he wouldn't.

She felt herself lapsing into raw panic, felt the darkness closing in on her, engulfing her. A tide of sobs, restrained too long now, welled up in her throat. She fought to keep from giving in to the hopelessness coursing through her, knowing one second of weakness, one errant tear, might bring on a fit of hysteria.

She couldn't risk losing control. Not for a moment. If he came for her, she would fight him. She had the knife. She had her will. She would fight.

How long had she been here, crouched down, huddled in the corner, in the darkness? Her legs ached. Her shoulders felt stiff and swollen from staying still for so long a time.

Gradually, Whitney became aware that outside the closet door something was happening. A change. Movement.

She tensed, drawing herself even tighter against the closet wall, her hands gripping her knees.

The knife! Where was it?

Frantic, she palmed the floor beside her, retrieved the knife, gripped it, waiting.

Suddenly, a silver strand of light ran across the bottom opening of the closet door. It disappeared, then returned, stopped, and held.

Without warning, the door exploded open. The beam of the flashlight shot through the closet, up, then to the floor. Clothes were jerked aside. The light swept, dropped, found her.

Blinded as the light froze her in its glare, Whitney threw up an arm to shield her eyes. Abruptly, the light swept away from her face. She felt hands grasping her shoulders, pulling her up to her feet, out of the corner, out of the closet.

She raised the knife, her hand trembling violently. With the knife slicing at the air, she felt an irrational rush of panic and for an instant squeezed her eyes shut.

She couldn't bear to see his face again.

A hand grabbed her wrist, pried the knife away from her.

Whitney opened her mouth and screamed.

Gentle hands now. Smoothing back her hair, wiping the tears from her cheeks, holding her, pulling her close . . .

"Michael?"

For one incredulous moment she stared at him. He tucked the flashlight, still burning, under his arm, and put his other hand to her hair, stroking it, trying to soothe her. His eyes glistened in the indirect beam of the flashlight, glinting with unmistakable anger and something else.

"Whitney—shh—it's all right now. It's all right. You're safe. What happened? I couldn't find you. I looked everywhere—"

Half sobbing, too weak with relief to answer, Whitney dug her fingers into his jacket and clung to him.

After a moment, he eased her away from him. He reached to prop the flashlight on the desk, then turned and took her by the shoulders.

"Are you hurt?" His face was hard, his features strained.

Whitney shook her head. "The lights . . . the power went out.

I woke up . . . it was dark . . . and I thought someone was here, in the house. . . ."

He put an arm around her, scooped up the flashlight, and gently helped her into the chair at the desk. He bent and tipped her chin up, so she could see his lips. "Candles?" he said. "Do you have candles in the house?"

Still dazed, Whitney stared at him, then shook her head. "Candles . . . yes . . . but no matches. I couldn't find the matches."

He put a hand to her arm, then indicated that she should wait for him. "I'll look. You stay here."

He returned shortly with a box of safety matches in one hand and a large, lighted candle in the other. "From the kitchen," he told her, pocketing the box and taking her hand to help her up. "Come on, let's get you to the couch. Then I'll collect more candles."

As she got to her feet, Whitney glimpsed her purse. It was lodged between the desk and the closet door. She simply hadn't looked far enough.

Michael helped her into the living room, waiting until she sat down before taking the flashlight and going in search of more candles. When he had lighted at least half a dozen more, he tossed some fresh logs onto the fireplace and made a fire, waiting until the flames blazed high to come and sit down beside her.

"Better?" he asked, settling himself on the cushion next to her and taking her hand.

Whitney nodded, grateful for the warm strength of his hand enfolding hers.

He didn't try to coax her to talk but simply sat in silence, watching her, occasionally giving her hand a reassuring squeeze. Whitney looked at her watch. It was almost five o'clock. Five o'clock in the morning.

She was still trembling, but the terror had finally begun to subside. "Why . . . did you come?" A thought struck Whitney, and she went rigid, dropping his hand. "H-how did you get in?"

Michael's gaze went to her hands, then back to her face. He studied her for a moment. "I came because of the lamp in the window."

At her frown, he explained. "I get up before dawn most days. It's the best time to work on my prints and get some writing done so I can use the daylight hours for shooting."

His eyes searched hers, but he made no move to touch her. "I realized something wasn't right when I woke up. I looked out and saw that the streetlight just across the way was off. Then I noticed the light in your office window wasn't on any longer. I decided to check." He paused, then added, "The power is off all the way down the block, just on this side. I called the power company and was told by one of the emergency crew that someone had vandalized a transformer."

Whitney glanced across the room to the entryway and the outside door. "But how did you get in?" She watched him.

He hesitated for a moment. "I, ah, I'm afraid I took advantage of those office locks I was complaining about the other day. The credit card bit, you know." He gave her a cryptic smile. "I did tell you they were worthless. Perhaps now you'll get them replaced."

Whitney looked away, suddenly embarrassed by the memory of how he had found her, huddled in the closet like a frightened child. And the way she had screamed when he opened the door . . .

A gentle hand cupped her chin and turned her toward him. "Whitney . . . it's all right now. No one's in the house—I searched it thoroughly before I found you."

Whitney felt her face burn. She hoped the candlelight was too dim to betray her humiliation.

Michael's features softened even more, and when he again reached for her hand, Whitney gave it willingly. "It must be an incredibly terrifying feeling . . . not being able to hear . . . or to see. I'm so sorry that happened to you."

"I thought it was—"

Michael nodded, not letting her finish. "You thought someone was in the house."

Whitney hadn't the slightest doubt that someone *had* been in the house. She had felt the corruption of his presence.

Michael dipped his head slightly, watching her. "Are you all right, *ma girsha?*"

He blinked, then smiled as his eyes went over her puzzled face. "It means, ah . . . *my girl.*" After a moment, he added, "It's a Gaelic—endearment."

Their eyes met and held for a long time. His smile turned almost regretful when he finally spoke. "Let me take you to Jennifer's. You need to get some sleep, and you mustn't be alone."

The memory of Jennifer's telephone message hit Whitney full force. She sat up and clutched his arm. "You don't know . . . about Daniel?"

He drew both her hands together and enfolded them between his. "I do, yes." At her frown, he explained. "I called their house after I left here tonight. I was thinking that perhaps I could drive out to the camp tomorrow—ah, what's it called—"

"Helping Hand?" she supplied.

"That's it, yes. It sounded like an interesting place to shoot, perhaps to do something in conjunction with the Friend-to-Friend Association. Actually, I was hoping you'd go with me. Jennifer took my call and told me what had happened."

"Then you know *how* it happened?"

He nodded. "And I expect you're blaming yourself, aren't you?"

Unnerved by his perception, Whitney didn't answer.

His hands tightened on hers. "Don't, Whitney. You're not responsible."

There was kindness in his eyes. But if he only knew . . .

He drew his face closer to hers. "You're exhausted. Get a coat, and I'll take you to the Kaines' so you can rest. You can't stay here."

Whitney shook her head, pulling her hands away.

"Whitney—"

Her eyes started to fill, but she wouldn't weep. She wouldn't. She had to hold together. "Don't . . . please. I can't go . . . up there. Not tonight." She would have to stay away from now on, of course. No matter how much she cared about them . . . *because* she cared about them.

Without touching her, he held her with his eyes. "You're sure?"

Nodding, she looked away. Jennifer would never understand, never stop trying to help. She couldn't put her at risk. She *wouldn't.*

When she turned back, Michael had left the couch and gone to stoke the fire. Whitney watched him, kneeling on the hearth, his back to her. All his movements were so precise, so capable. What must he think of her? That she was emotionally unstable? Ill? How pathetic she must appear to him, a man who had probably never doubted himself in his life. Was it pity she had seen in his eyes tonight? The thought hit her like a blow, sickening her.

He returned, again dropping down beside her, closer this time. "All right, then, if you won't be moved, the two of us will share a sunrise." He glanced down at his watch. "And soon, at that."

He leaned back, drawing Whitney inside the shelter of his arm while settling her head gently against his shoulder.

Whitney hesitated for only a moment before letting herself relax against his strength, trying not to think about anything else except that he was going to stay with her until the darkness had passed.

In some way she couldn't begin to understand, he seemed to know instinctively that, at least for now, she needed nothing quite so much as she needed a friend. Obviously, he was offering to be that friend.

And Whitney needed him too much to turn him away.

He reached a hand to cup her chin, turning her face to his so she could read his lips. His eyes were kind but determined. "Tell me about it, Whitney. It's too big for you to go on carrying alone. Talk to me."

THIRTEEN

WHITNEY was still talking when the first pale light of dawn cautiously threaded its way around the drapes and through the windowpanes.

The anguish she would have expected to feel at the replaying of that nightmarish year of her life hadn't come. Instead, there had been an unexpected feeling of catharsis, an easing of the pain. She wondered if it would have been the same with anyone other than Michael.

He had simply sat there, listening quietly, holding her hand through the entire story, watching her, and encouraging her.

If his features had appeared grim and taut as she spoke, there was at least no condemnation, no apparent contempt for the naïveté revealed by her tale. He seemed to understand and accept how a far more gullible Whitney might have become infatuated with a deceptive Louisville health club instructor.

She had first met Cory Ross upon enrolling in a self-defense course at a health club. He was the instructor and was new in town, having moved to Louisville only two months earlier. He asked Whitney for a date after the first class. She refused, but he kept on asking until he broke down her reserve.

On their first date, they had attended a church praise festival. He professed to be a Christian, and Whitney believed him—at first.

Only later was she to learn that he was brilliantly deceitful and hopelessly insane.

"You said he was an actor," Michael put in. "What kind of an actor?"

"Amateur groups," Whitney explained. "Community theater. He was just getting . . . involved in one of the local players groups when we met. He said it was only a hobby . . . an 'enrichment' experience. But he took it seriously. Far more seriously than he would ever admit."

Whitney wondered at the flinty edge in Michael's expression when he nodded. "You were attracted to him then?"

Whitney thought about her reply. "I don't know if you can understand this or not . . . I'm not sure *I* understand it . . . but Cory appeared to be completely . . . normal. He looked like the typical . . . boy next door. The captain of the football team. The son of your mother's best friend."

"Actually, that's a common sort of description for stalkers," Michael said grimly. "And sociopaths. Were you in love with him?" he asked bluntly, watching her.

Whitney looked away. "No. Fascinated, maybe, but not in love. I'd never known anyone . . . quite like Cory. He was clever. Intelligent. Unconventional. And he had only been in Louisville a couple of months." She turned back to him. "I suppose I was trying to be kind, at first."

His mouth thinned. "You'd do yourself an enormous service, Whitney, if you'd learn to curb your humanitarian instincts a bit."

Anger flared in Whitney. With an effort, she suppressed it, saying nothing. He didn't understand, she reminded herself. Michael was a loner. She had already seen his confusion in the midst of a crowd, and his solitary life was apparently a matter of choice.

He was the one who finally resumed the conversation. "After you realized he wasn't what he seemed, you tried to break it off?"

In spite of the fire blazing a few feet away, Whitney felt cold. She rubbed her arms, watching the flames lap at the logs in the fireplace. "He became intensely . . . jealous. He seemed to be . . . obsessed with me. If he called my apartment and I didn't answer, he'd come over and stand in the hall, leaning on the doorbell, pounding on the door."

She took a deep breath, then went on. "Once I was there, inside the apartment . . . but when my signal light flashed and I saw him through the peephole, I didn't open the door. I was frightened of him by then. I called Keith—a friend from school. He came over right away and told Cory to leave." Whitney rubbed her arms even harder. "Cory left. But not before he hit Keith hard enough to break his nose."

She lifted a hand and dragged it through her hair. For an instant she met Michael's eyes, then looked away. "I called him at the health club the next day . . . told him if he didn't stop, I was going to the police. He just laughed at me. He hadn't . . . laid a hand on me, he said, so what could the police do?"

"All too true, unfortunately," Michael said, his mouth hard.

"I knew he had a . . . temper," Whitney went on. "But at first I didn't pay much attention to his threats. I thought he'd give up once he saw I wasn't going to be . . . intimidated by him. I didn't return his calls, and I stopped going to the health club. I was hoping if I put enough distance between us, he'd just . . . forget about me."

She felt a tremor in her voice as she continued. "But he started harassing me continually after that. I'd come home and find my front door open, my dresser drawers emptied on the floor. Broken dishes in the kitchen, broken lamps . . ."

She shuddered as she continued. "He knew that I had a horror of . . . spiders. And bees. I started finding them—dozens of them—in my kitchen cabinets, in the canisters. . . ."

Her words drifted off, and Michael made no attempt to prompt her but merely wrapped both of her hands in his, waiting.

"At the time," Whitney continued, "I was teaching a night class for deaf adults at the high school. I would come out of the building after class, and he would be waiting for me—around the corner or in the parking lot. He would jump out at me like some sort of . . . wild thing. Being deaf . . . only made it harder for me, because I never had any warning." She drew in a shaky breath. "He liked to frighten me. Sometimes he'd wear those awful masks, the kind you buy at Halloween."

She sat unmoving, staring into the fire. When she finally turned back to Michael, she was unable to read the look in his eyes.

"One night," she went on, "he was . . . in the parking lot, waiting for me. He was dressed in his own clothes, and he seemed . . . normal. He begged me to go somewhere with him—to talk, he said. When I refused, he exploded."

Even now, the memory chilled her. Cory's face had distorted into a thundercloud, rage burning in his eyes. "He tried to force me into the car. When I fought him, he went . . . crazy. He was like an animal. He threw me . . . against the car, onto the ground. . . ."

She couldn't finish. Michael squeezed her hands but remained silent. Whitney closed her eyes for a moment, then opened them. "He started beating on me . . . pounding at me with his fists . . . kicking me. All the time, he was . . . awful things . . . and he forced me to read his lips, so I would know. . . ."

She stopped and lifted her eyes to Michael. "He was strong. He worked out all the time, knew karate—" She felt her voice go to a whisper. "It *hurt*. I didn't know anything could hurt like that. My parents had never even spanked me when I was a child. I didn't know what it was like to be hurt that way."

Her pulse hammering, Whitney realized suddenly that it was her own agony she saw burning out of Michael's eyes—as if he were taking the blows with her, for her. He lifted her hands and brushed his lips over her knuckles as if he could somehow heal the ugly memories simply by touching her.

". . . I don't remember anything else," she went on, "not until I woke up in the hospital. Apparently, the night custodian had seen us. He called the police, then ran outside to help me."

The sting of anguish in her eyes thickened to tears, and Michael pulled her into his arms.

"Cory . . . almost killed Mr. Johnson—the custodian— before the police got there. He beat him—he beat him almost to death." Whitney's voice broke on a sob, and she struggled to regain control.

Michael eased her away just enough that she could read his lips. "They locked Ross up, then?"

Whitney nodded. "In a state hospital . . . for the criminally insane."

Michael searched her eyes. "But now you think he's out?"

Whitney gripped his hands hard. "I *know* he's out, Michael! I know it! He's here. Don't ask me . . . how. But he's *here!*"

He smoothed her tousled hair and wiped a smudge from her cheek with his thumb. "So it seems."

Whitney tried to stop the trembling that had begun anew. "My parents have been in Florida . . . but they're due back in Louis- ville sometime next week. I'll have them check . . . through the prosecutor's office to verify it. But I *know* he's out."

"The local police will be able to get more information on him than your parents could," Michael told her. "And we're going to talk with them first thing this morning. You have to give them all the details."

Whitney nodded reluctantly. "I'll tell them," she sighed. "I suppose . . . I have no choice now."

"Not if you ever want to be free of him."

Free. The word brought a choking sob to Whitney's throat. Cory was the one who was free. She was the prisoner.

"I know you're right. But do you think the police will still be willing to keep it quiet? At least for now?"

"I expect they'll *want* it kept quiet—they'll have a better chance of capturing Ross if he thinks they're ignorant of his whereabouts. You're still worried about the Kaines, aren't you?"

"Yes. Surely you can understand why."

"I do, but I doubt that you'll be able to hold Jennifer off very long. She seems nothing if not persistent."

"I'll just . . . stay away from them," Whitney said, hating the thought. "At least until—"

Until what? Whitney couldn't finish. She wasn't sure she really believed there would ever be an end to the nightmare.

"You'll find it very difficult, won't you—avoiding the Kaines? You care a great deal about them, don't you?"

Whitney studied him. "Yes, I do. I . . . need them in my life. But you don't understand that, do you?"

His mouth thinned. "I suppose not."

Was he really as hard, as self-contained as he appeared to be, Whitney wondered? Somehow she didn't think so. "Haven't you ever . . . needed anyone, Michael?" she asked gently. "Hasn't there ever been anyone . . . important to you?"

She saw him withdraw from her, saw the shutters slam shut. He released her hands and got up from the couch, turning away. When he finally faced her again, his eyes were shadowed with pain.

"I had a sister," he said.

Whitney looked at him.

"She's dead."

Whitney's heart clenched. She got to her feet, wanting to touch him, yet uncertain as to whether she should. "What happened, Michael?"

He hesitated. When he finally answered, his pain was palpable. "Sile and I were orphans, actually. Our parents died in a railway accident when we were children. Sile was only four at the time. After that, it was a series of foster homes."

He glanced into the fire, then turned back to Whitney. "I was six years older than my sister, and when I came of age, I took custody of her. I did my best to give her a home, but it was—difficult." A muscle at the corner of his mouth tightened. "I was just getting settled with the constabulary. I had almost no free time to spend with Sile, and she was still so young. She needed a real family—security, stability—all the things I couldn't quite manage. My own life was chaotic enough as it was."

Whitney eased herself back to the couch, watching him as he went on. "The longer I was with the force, the more torn I became. While I was trying to figure out what to do with the rest of my life, Sile got herself mixed up with one of the extremist guerrilla outfits. She was a born rebel, you see."

His face softened for just an instant, and he even managed a ghost of a smile. "She was always in the fray for a free Ireland. She was bright, brave, intense—all the lads were wild for her. She could have done anything, been anything, she set her mind to. Instead—" For the first time since he'd begun, he faltered. "Instead," he went on, his features set in stone, "she ended up dead on the Falls Road. A bomb. It needn't have happened. She ran out into the street to try and help one of her friends. The bomb killed them both and three others."

And she was all you had, Whitney thought. Again she stood and put a hand to his arm.

His eyes were fierce when he looked at her. "She was a lot like you. She insisted on thrusting herself into everyone else's life, taking on their problems, even going to war for them. And it killed her."

Whitney shrank inwardly from the look of anguish in his eyes. "Oh, Michael . . . I'm so sorry. She sounds . . . wonderful."

His face went rigid. "She was. Wonderful—and very, very foolish."

His life had been hard. But his heart wasn't. Whitney suddenly knew that much about Michael Devlin—even if he didn't. "Is that when you left Belfast?"

He glanced at her hand on his arm, then expelled a long breath. "No, not right away. It took me a bit longer to realize that I didn't want to spend the rest of my life as a hired gun pretending to be a policeman."

He placed his hands on her shoulders and gave her a rueful smile. "We're very different, you and I, Whitney. You've spent your life doing for other people, and I've spent most of mine *avoiding* them."

Whitney could feel the strength in his hands on her shoulders, could sense the power of the man himself. Yet she somehow knew there was a gentleness in him, a gentleness he didn't seem to recognize or want to acknowledge.

"You told Daniel that you're a Christian," she ventured. "I don't understand . . . how you can be . . . indifferent to other people and still be a Christian."

The warmth in his gaze flickered out, and he released her. "You think *God* isn't sometimes indifferent to his people?" he said bitterly.

A mixture of pain and anger burned out from his eyes. "Let me tell you something. I've seen God's people blown to bits in the middle of a Belfast street by bombs that weren't even meant for them. I've seen a child shot down in front of his own home because his father didn't happen to believe what the fellow behind the gun thought he should believe. I can tell you about entire families assassinated by a gang of teens who didn't even know the names of their victims—or why they were sent to kill them."

His jaw tightened still more. "That's Northern Ireland. But what about here in the States? What's so different here? Street gangs rioting and violating. People killing children—child abuse, abortion. The homeless living in cardboard boxes in the depths of winter while churches spend their millions on bigger buildings and posh pews."

His face was a mask of bitterness. "Tell me God doesn't turn away from his people, Whitney. Go ahead—pick up your morning newspaper, and then tell me God still cares."

So much pain in him . . . so much anger. Oh, Michael . . . Michael, what would it take to heal your heart?

"It isn't . . . God who's turned away," she said. "It's the rest of us." Suddenly exhausted, far too drained to match his intensity, Whitney shook her head. "I don't have any answers, Michael. Everything you said is true. I know what's happening. In Ireland, in America— everywhere, all over the world. And one person alone can't change it. But one person . . . and then another person . . . and another . . . that can make a difference. It's Christ who makes the difference in us . . . so we can make a difference for the people around us. God hasn't turned away, Michael. It's just that we . . . can't see enough of the picture to understand what he's doing."

He stared down at her, lifting a hand to touch her hair. "You're a good person, Whitney. I only wish you weren't such a danger to yourself."

He crossed his arms over his chest. "I suppose you're going to insist on going to church this morning. Even though you haven't slept and you have no electricity."

When Whitney nodded, he inclined his head in resignation. "Then we'll talk with the police afterward. I'll go along now if you're sure you'll be all right."

"Michael?"

He lifted a brow. His eyes were tired, she noticed, and for once he didn't look quite as confident and in control.

"You said you were . . . going to be my shadow, remember?"

He nodded, waiting.

"Does that mean you'll be at church this morning, too?"

He gave her a look of grudging, but faintly amused, respect. "I expect I will," he replied, then turned to go.

FOURTEEN

JENNIFER sat at her desk late the following Tuesday morning, her office door closed, her studio monitor off, her heart heavy.

Turning away from the window, she rested her elbows on the desk, framing her face with her hands. She couldn't quite grasp how her life could have changed so much so quickly.

Without anger or censure, she honed in on the two people responsible for the change: Daniel and Whitney. Her husband and her friend.

Whitney had been peculiar for days now. It was understandable that she would be guarded and anxious after that awful attack at the festival; no one would have expected anything else. But without question Whitney had begun acting especially odd since the arrival of Michael Devlin.

Jennifer knew that Whitney was avoiding *her;* that much was clear, even if the reason was not. Oh, she had been noticeably concerned about Daniel's accident when they talked at church Sunday morning. But she had declined an invitation to drop by later that afternoon, offering no excuse.

Then the stone-faced Devlin had shown up, cornering Whitney after the service for what had appeared to be a very serious discussion. They had walked outside together, his hand on Whitney's arm in a gesture that looked almost possessive.

When Whitney hadn't so much as called the house or the station by Monday afternoon, Jennifer called her. It had been an unsatisfying and unsettling conversation.

Her every attempt to coax Whitney to come by for a visit had been met with evasion. Even when she pressed, commenting that Daniel "could use some cheering up," Whitney had still backed off from a definite commitment.

Later in the day, Lee Kelsey, one of the station's disc jockeys, innocently remarked that he had seen Whitney and "that Irish guy" at Simpson's coffee shop the evening before. Jennifer had felt a momentary sting of rejection, hurt that Whitney could make time for the photojournalist but not for her friends.

When she complained to Daniel, his attitude left her feeling even worse.

"Jennifer, you're not being objective about Whitney," he said. "And you're being absolutely unfair to Devlin."

She had been sure that Daniel, of all people, would understand her feelings. His unexpected disagreement made her miserable.

"Whitney's a normal, unattached young woman, and this man is single, new in town, and apparently interested in her." He spoke with forced patience, as if he were explaining something that should be easily discernible to a child. "Why *wouldn't* Whitney opt to spend an evening with him instead of coming up here to sit around with us and discuss my broken leg?" he added sourly.

Daniel, of course, was Jennifer's *real* problem.

The uncharacteristic streak of sullenness that had surfaced in her husband over the past few days had tilted Jennifer's world off its axis.

She had never, *ever* seen Daniel pout. But that didn't change the reality that Daniel was, indeed, *pouting*.

Up until yesterday, Jennifer had dismissed his withdrawal and surliness as no more than could be expected. This morning, however, by the time she had gotten Jason onto the school bus and picked up most of the clutter from the previous day, she knew she could no longer ignore the morose fog in which Daniel had wrapped himself ever since the accident.

He had been sitting in his dilapidated old recliner, seemingly unaware of her presence in the room.

"Lee Kelsey is going to finish my afternoon drive time for me so I can come home early today," Jennifer began hopefully. "I thought maybe you'd like to go for a ride later."

"That's not even a possibility," he muttered after a moment. "There's no way I can get comfortable in that Honda with—this." He flicked a hand over the top of his cast, managing a look of distaste even with his eyes closed. "And the station's new van hasn't come in yet."

"Oh. I didn't think of that." Jennifer decided to try another approach. "Well, I know what we *can* do," she said brightly. "Let's have your mother and dad over for dinner tonight. I'm in the mood for some company."

He didn't answer. "Daniel?" she prompted. "Would you like that?"

"Jennifer," he said after a long, deep sigh, "please stop trying to entertain me. It isn't necessary."

Jennifer bit her lower lip and shoved her hands into the pockets of her robe. "How do you feel, Daniel?"

He shrugged. "OK."

"Is your leg bothering you?"

"No, it's fine." He stirred restlessly in the chair, as if trying to maneuver himself into a comfortable position.

"You're not in any pain?"

Daniel opened his eyes, and Jennifer thought she sensed a small flicker of impatience cross his features. But he merely shook his head. "No," he said tightly, "at least, not now."

Jennifer went to stand a little closer to him. "Then what's wrong?"

"Wrong?"

"If you're not in any pain, and if your leg isn't bothering you, then what *is* bothering you?"

He drummed the fingers of his left hand on the chair arm. "Bothering me?"

"Don't do that! You know it *irritates* me."

He looked genuinely surprised. "Don't do what?"

"That! Don't answer my questions by asking your own. You always do that when you won't admit you know exactly what I mean."

"But I *don't* know what you mean," he said with maddening calm as he resumed his finger-thumping.

"Daniel, you have been a *stone* for days now, ever since you broke your leg! You don't talk to me; you don't even smile at me. I might as well be a—a *chair* for all the reaction I get from you!"

He straightened slightly, lifted his chin a fraction, and, much to her relief, stopped tapping his fingers. "I'm sorry. I didn't realize."

"I shouldn't have said anything," Jennifer said. "I know this is awful for you."

Quickly, he shook his head, waving away her attempted apology. "No, I'm sure I haven't been very good company."

"Daniel, I'm not expecting you to be good company. I'm just concerned because you don't usually—"

Pout. She had almost said it. Biting her lip even harder, she went to him. She squeezed his shoulder, then bent to kiss him on the forehead. "I just feel frustrated because I don't know how to help you."

His expression gentled, and he pulled Jennifer down beside him on the arm of the chair. "No, you're right. I've been rotten."

He sighed again and shifted slightly in the chair. "I feel like such a lump," he said, his expression still glum. "You're doing everything for me—even more than usual—and I can't do any-

thing about it except sit here, congealing in this chair. I can't walk;
I can't swim—I can't do anything but make life more difficult for
you."

"Daniel, you *know* I don't mind doing things for you!"

"I know. But *I* mind."

Anger surged anew in Jennifer as she considered the extreme
cruelty that had been inflicted upon her husband by someone
who most likely would never know—or care about—the extent
of the damage he had caused.

Again she kissed him, this time on his bearded cheek. "Daniel,"
she said softly, "I *do* understand. I really do. I just wish there were
something I could do to make things easier for you."

He had squeezed her hand then and even managed a small
smile, but he made it clear that the discussion was at an end.

So now Jennifer sat at her desk, her thoughts locked on her
husband's depression—and her own. At the back of her mind, the
puzzle of Whitney's odd behavior nagged at her, but she simply
couldn't deal with anything else right now. First she had to think
of some way to help Daniel.

She glanced at her watch. It was almost time to set up for
her afternoon show, and she hadn't called Daniel's mother
about dinner yet. It occurred to her as she dialed that perhaps
she might attach a plea for help to her dinner invitation. Pauline Kaine was a wise woman, and she might have some insight
or advice to offer.

After leaving word with the school secretary for Pauline to call
her, Jennifer walked to the studio, put on her headset, and waited
for her cue. She felt better already. As the light went on, she
forced a cheerful tone over the lump in her throat and opened
her mike.

"Hello, everybody. It's twelve-thirty in Shepherd Valley. This is
Jennifer Kaine, and I've got some Good News for you. . . ."

Half dozing, Daniel heard a key turn in the front door even before Sunny barked. He stirred and shook his head, vaguely aware that he had slept through the last part of Jennifer's show.

He listened to Sunny pad over to the front door, no longer barking, but now whining with excitement.

"Daniel? It's just me, dear." The door closed. "Yes, Sunny, I see you, too. Want your ears rubbed, do you?"

"Mom?" Daniel sat up and wiped a hand over his eyes. "What are you doing here?"

"School's out. It's almost three."

He felt a rush of air as she breezed up to him and planted a kiss on top of his head. "I just thought I'd stop in and get the spaghetti sauce started for Jennifer. Jason's not home yet?"

Daniel breathed in the familiar scent of her perfume and again shook his head. "The bus doesn't come until almost four." He yawned. "If Jennifer talked you into making the sauce, that must mean you and Dad are coming to dinner."

"We are indeed. And I'm looking forward to it. This family has had precious little time together lately, it seems to me. As soon as your sister and Gabe get back, I'm going to have all of you over for lasagna."

"You won't have to ask twice."

He listened to his mother's brisk steps as she crossed the living room and dining room, then entered the kitchen. The three rooms were undivided by walls, so she talked to him as she worked.

"Jennifer still doesn't trust her sauce," she said distractedly, "though I don't understand why."

"I think she's just intimidated by yours." He smiled a little to himself. "With good reason."

"Jennifer's a very good cook, Daniel. You shouldn't tease her."

Daniel stretched, then dropped his hands onto the arms of the chair and listened. His mother even *sounded* efficient when she cooked, he thought. Jennifer usually banged and clanged and occasionally crashed. His mother clicked and hummed and whirred, singing softly as she worked.

He leaned back against the chair. The sounds coming from the kitchen were oddly comforting, and for a moment he felt almost guilty, as if he were somehow betraying Jennifer.

It's called regression, Kaine. It's a lot easier to reminisce about the good old days than to deal with the grim reality of the present.

"Daniel?" Apparently, his mother had asked him a question.

"Sorry, Mom. What?"

"I asked if you want me to make some coffee."

He nodded. "That sounds good."

Soon she returned and set a tray on the table beside him. "Here we are. I found some cookies in the jar, too," she said, gently guiding his hand to the tray.

He heard her sit down on the couch across from him. "Thanks, Mom."

"Eat some cookies. You look a little thin, Daniel."

He couldn't stop a grin. "Mom, I've been a lump for four days now. My total physical activity has consisted of picking up a fork and opening my mouth. There's no possible way I could look thin."

"Still—"

"I'll eat the cookies."

He pictured her in his mind, perched forward, tall and trim, her hands clasped quietly in her lap. Her dark, warm eyes would be fastened on him with a combination of motherly concern and discomfiting sharpness.

"Jennifer's a wonderful girl, Daniel. Do you know how blessed you are?"

Surprised, he set his cup down. "Of course I know. What brought that on?"

"You're depressed, aren't you, Daniel?" Her tone was sympathetic.

He groaned.

"What is it, dear? The pain?"

He expelled a long breath, suppressing his impatience. "No, I'm fine, Mom. Really."

"But you *are* depressed."

"No," Daniel said defensively. "I know about depression. This isn't depression."

"I see. What is it then, dear? What's wrong?"

"*Nothing's* wrong, Mom. What would you and Jennifer like me to do? Hop around and wave my crutch in the air to show how much I'm enjoying all this?"

His face grew hot in the silence. "Sorry," he said quietly. "That was uncalled for."

"It's all right," she said after a moment of silence. "I understand. But you're right, Daniel. You're not depressed."

He took a sip of coffee, relieved at warding off a maternal lecture.

"You're feeling sorry for yourself."

The coffee stopped halfway down his throat, burning all the way. Mother or not, he'd just about had his limit of women analyzing his emotions. He wouldn't argue, of course. One of the first lessons Lucas Kaine had taught both his children was that neither of them, for any reason, was ever to argue with "my wife." In matters of discipline, Daniel remembered wryly, he and Lyss had always had a surefire way of measuring their father's mood: If he referred to their mother as "my wife," it was heavy stuff. A closed case.

"I know about feeling sorry for yourself, Daniel. I know exactly what you're feeling."

When he would have disputed her words, she stopped him. "You wouldn't remember—you were only a baby—a few months old. But you've heard your father and me talk about that awful time I had to spend in a sanitarium. When I had tuberculosis."

He had forgotten. Any reference to his mother's earlier illness had always been brief and quickly dismissed by his father, who never seemed to want to talk about it.

"There I was, a year out of college, a young wife, a new mother with a baby son. And I had to leave everything—you, your father, our home—to go and stay in that awful hospital." She stopped, and there was a rare tremor in her voice when she added, "I was terrified. Absolutely terrified."

Daniel leaned forward, his interest captured. This was something he'd never heard much about. Neither parent ever gave the experience more than a passing word, an unpleasant frown of remembrance. For the first time he wondered what it had been like for her.

"How long did you have to stay in the hospital?"

"Months." She uttered a short, dry laugh. "It might just as well have been years. I *mourned,* Daniel. I actually mourned for you and your father, as if you were dead to me. I worried constantly about whether or not you'd even remember me when I came home. I worried about whether your father would still love me. I became almost obsessively anxious about our marriage. It was so painful, knowing I was missing your first words and your first steps—all those wonderful firsts that mean so much to a mother."

"Grandpa Dan and Grandma Lou took care of me, didn't they?"

"Yes, and I don't know what Lucas would have done without them. He was just setting up his practice when I got sick." Her voice was low and shaky. "It was a *terrible* time in our lives."

She sighed deeply, then went on. "The worst part of the entire ordeal, for me, was knowing that your grandmother was doing all the things *I* wanted to be doing. Not that I resented her for it—I loved her like my own mother—but I felt so *guilty.* There she was, trying to manage her own work and mine as well. I *hated* that! It made me feel so *useless*. And so helpless."

"But it got better?" he prompted gently.

"It wouldn't have if your Grandpa Dan hadn't written me a very important letter."

Daniel could hear the faint smile of remembrance in her voice as she went on. "Your father had confided in him—poor man, he had to unload on *someone*. Anyway, your grandfather Dan wrote me this wonderful letter that simply overflowed with love—and a whole storehouse of wisdom."

She stopped for a moment, and Daniel heard her rise from the couch and walk in the direction of the fireplace.

"He understood. Your grandfather was always keenly sensitive to others. He explained to me how it was with your grandmother—that taking care of you and Lucas wasn't a burden but a blessing for her, that she was happiest when she was pouring herself out for others. He said that if it hadn't been you and Lucas who needed her, she would have been spending herself on someone else. That was just her way, he said. Her nature. And I knew he was right."

Daniel squirmed a little, beginning to sense her point.

"And that's your Jennifer's way, Daniel," she said quietly, coming back to put a hand on his shoulder. "Jennifer could no more feel burdened by doing things for you or Jason—or for anyone else—than she could stop loving you. Your dear wife has so much love to give that she's always looking for new ways to give it."

Daniel's throat tightened as he felt her squeeze his shoulder. "It's just as your Grandpa Dan said, dear. People like your grandmother and Jennifer are those who make *love* an active verb. They have a servant's heart. It's as natural for them to do for others as breathing. What's difficult for the rest of us is to *receive*. We get so caught up in self-pity and pride—and our determination to be self-sufficient—that we don't see that we're actually rejecting their love. Sometimes, Daniel," she said thoughtfully, "you love *best* by accepting the love of others."

Daniel felt a dawning recognition begin somewhere deep inside him. Nothing she had said was new. He had heard it before, knew it in his heart. But it had always been so difficult for him to acknowledge his own needs, even with Jennifer. The fact was, though, that he did need her—desperately. He just had to accept that need . . . and her willingness to give.

He covered his mother's hand on his shoulder with his own, and she bent to touch her cheek to his. "Daniel, let your wife love you. Right now, you need to take. And Jennifer needs to give. Don't throw her love back at her. Don't you see, dear, that the greatest hurt you can inflict on her is to reject what she's trying to offer? Don't do that to her, Daniel."

Not waiting for a reply, she gave him a hug, then kissed him once more on the forehead. "I have to run, dear. Your father and I want to stop at the nursing home and look in on Aunt Serena before we come over tonight."

"Mom—"

"Tell Jennifer the sauce is all done except for a little more oregano later. I left the heat—oh, here she comes now."

Daniel heard the key turn in the door and eagerly leaned forward at the sound of Jennifer's voice.

"I hope that wonderful smell coming out of my kitchen is what I think it is."

"It is, dear," his mother replied, "but if I don't get out of here, I'm not going to be back in time to enjoy the fruits of my labor."

Daniel listened impatiently as the two women drew out their good-byes. Finally the door closed, and Jennifer came to graze his cheek with a hesitant kiss.

He reached out a hand to her, drawing her down beside him. "I missed you," he told her.

"Is something wrong, Daniel?" Her voice was guarded.

"No, nothing's wrong," he said quietly. "Not now."

Sensing her confusion in the silence, he pulled her closer and wrapped her in his arms.

"Daniel, I might hurt your leg—"

"The leg's fine. Forget the leg." He lifted a heavy wave of hair and let it sift slowly through his fingers.

"Daniel, are you sure everything is all right—"

"Everything is very much all right." He kissed her. Soundly.

Afterward, she pulled in a long, shaky breath. "I'm glad you're feeling better, darling."

He laughed. "I've been that bad, huh?" He paused. "I'm going to need your help. If you don't mind."

"Anything, Daniel."

He smiled at the pleased note he heard in her voice. "I know you'll be busy tonight, with the folks coming over and all. But I thought maybe tomorrow morning, before you go in to the station, you might help me set up at the piano instead of in this chair. I've got the music for a new song going through my head," he explained, "and I'd like to start working on it."

She hugged him tightly around the neck, and he could hear the relief in her voice. "Oh, I'm *glad,* Daniel! Of course I'll help you. I'd *love* to help you!"

"I thought you would," he said softly, burying his face in the sweet silk of her hair.

"What kind of song is it, Daniel?"

He smiled. "I'm pretty sure it's going to be a love song, darlin'."

FIFTEEN

B Y eight-thirty Wednesday morning, Whitney had five people in her office: two wheelchair-bound members of Friend-to-Friend; their two drivers— teenagers from the local Christian high school who served as volunteers under a work-study project; and Stephanie Lowe, a county social worker who needed Whitney's testimony in an upcoming hearing on an abuse case involving a disabled child.

She also had a leak in the office. Something had given way in the ancient, unused bathroom upstairs, causing a narrow but persistent stream of water to break through the ceiling only a few feet away from her desk. So far, she had managed to control it with buckets and a plastic shower liner. She continued to hope for a free moment to call the plumber.

Added to this was a phone that had been jammed for over thirty minutes with messages scurrying across the display, each demanding immediate attention.

The entire day was already out of control. Given the fact that she hadn't slept for two nights, Whitney sensed impending disaster.

And when Michael Devlin walked in, her rioting emotions only added to the chaos.

Whitney was bent over her desk signing travel vouchers for the drivers when the door opened. She saw Michael stop and take in the room, his expression going from curiosity to amused incredulity.

His gaze shifted from the drivers to the impatiently tapping foot of the caseworker, then locked on the plastic runner on which buckets were lined up like a small brigade of galvanized guards.

He glanced upward from the buckets to the stained ceiling, finally turning his attention to Whitney. "This, ah, might not be the best time to talk with you?"

Straightening, Whitney lifted a hand to indicate that he should wait, then gave each of the drivers a check. With a smile, she fended off the mischievous Jonathan Kaylor's weekly attempt to flirt with her as he wheeled his chair down the ramp.

Behind Kaylor was Becky Price. A cerebral palsy victim confined to a wheelchair for most of her twenty-five years, Becky had a smile people remembered forever and a warmth even the coldest of hearts couldn't resist.

Whitney gave her a quick hug before closing the door and turning to the fiery-haired caseworker already on her feet and headed toward the desk.

"Whitney, here are the notes you said you wanted for the hearing Friday," she said, her words spilling out in a rush as she stared at Whitney over the rim of her glasses. "I tried to give you an idea of what type of questions to expect, but be prepared for anything. We're dealing with a defense attorney who's a crazy man and a prosecutor whose metabolism runs on leaded fuel only." She looked down at the file in her hands and shrugged.

"Stephanie . . . slow down, please," Whitney interrupted.

The case worker glanced up. "What? Oh, sorry, your eyes can't keep up with my mouth, huh? Understandable. What's wrong, Whitney?" she asked, peering sharply over her glasses. "You look tired."

Reaching for the file, Whitney smiled at her. "I'm fine. Things have been . . . hectic."

Stephanie nodded, thrusting the file at Whitney. "I know hectic. Listen, I have to run. I've got an adoption hearing at nine."

"Wait a minute," Whitney said, picking up a small piece of memo paper. "I had a message on my machine yesterday. It came in while I was at lunch—apparently from someone at the Social Services Office." Whitney handed her the note. "They want me to make a call on this man today. Do you know anything about it? The message said it's urgent."

The social worker glanced at the note. Shaking her head, she handed the message back to Whitney. "I don't know who called, but you'll probably be wasting your time. We've had a couple of investigators out there over the past year, and they got zilch. From everything I've heard, old Tom Power is a dedicated hermit. What are they wanting you to do, sweet-talk him into accepting some help? They're probably worried he's starving to death up there on top of his mountain." Without giving Whitney time to respond, she asked, "Are you going?"

"I suppose so," Whitney answered uncertainly. "I can at least try."

"Brave girl. Let me know if you get anywhere."

When the signal for the telephone flashed, Stephanie backed off with a quick wave. "I'll get out of your hair. Thanks, Whitney. I'll call you." Brushing Michael's arm on the way out, she charged out of the office at a run.

Whitney started to answer the phone, shooting a harried smile of apology in Michael's direction. He grinned at her and walked the rest of the way into the room. "Go ahead," he told her, gesturing toward the phone as he perched on the side of her desk to wait.

The display lighted as soon as she lifted the handset and said hello.

"Whitney, it's Jennifer."

Caught off guard for a moment, Whitney stared blankly down at the display. Then, recovering, she began to type in her reply, so the relay operator could take over. "How are you, Jennifer? And Daniel—how's he feeling?"

"Daniel's doing fine, but I could use a friend." There was a pause. "Where have you been?"

"I—I knew you'd be . . . busy," Whitney typed, "with Daniel's accident and all."

"I've missed you, Whitney. Listen, Daniel and I were wondering if you'd come to dinner Saturday night? Jason's begging to see you."

Whitney fumbled for the words. "Saturday night? Well, I . . ."

"We thought you might like to ask Michael Devlin to come, too."

Startled, Whitney looked at him. His brows shot up in a questioning look.

"We'd love to have you both," Jennifer went on. "Are you having a busy day? I thought maybe you could stop by the station later, and we'd go to lunch."

Whitney was tempted. She missed their lunches, their talks . . . their friendship. But she typed in the words she thought were best. "I'm sorry, Jennifer, I can't today. I have to drive out to—" she glanced down at the note still in her hand— "Blackwater Run early this afternoon."

Michael's hand covered hers as he gave her a look that clearly said he knew her response had caused her pain.

There was a pause, then, "Blackwater Run? That's almost ten miles out, Whitney—and straight up the side of a mountain. Why are you going up there?"

Whitney typed an explanation about Thomas Power and the request for a contact.

Jennifer's response was immediate. "Do you know how to get there?"

"Vaguely. I know it's close to the campground."

Jennifer gave her directions, then paused again. "Are you going out there alone?"

Whitney was unable to stop a smile. Even over an LCD display, Jennifer's protective instincts came through. "Yes, Jennifer," she typed in.

"Whitney, Tom Power has an awful reputation. Everybody says he's a stubborn, cantankerous, grouchy old man."

"Sounds as if he'll fit right in with the rest of my day," Whitney responded. "Relax, Jennifer. I've encountered crusty old men before."

"I wish I didn't have to jock the afternoon show. I'd ride out there with you."

"I'll just threaten to send you out next time if he gives me any trouble. Jennifer, I really have to go—it's a circus here this morning."

After an instant, Jennifer's reply came back. "You won't forget about Saturday night?"

"I'll call you back on it, all right?"

She hung up and looked at Michael. He placed his hand on hers, and he was studying her face with a look that made her feel special.

Dipping his head a little closer, he said, "Please tell me this is not a routine morning in your life. I'd hate to believe that you start every day like this."

Caught for a moment in the magnetic field of his eyes, Whitney reluctantly eased her hand away from his, dragging it through her hair. His eyes followed the movement, then returned to her face.

"No," she replied with a weak laugh. "Sometimes it's worse."

Still leaning close, he watched her. "And you didn't sleep last night either, did you?"

"I—"

He wagged a finger at her. "Don't ever try to lie, Whitney Sharyn. Not with those eyes."

She smiled sheepishly. "Jennifer asked us to dinner," she told him, trying to divert his attention.

He smiled at her. "Jennifer asked *me* to dinner? You're sure that wasn't somebody else hacking into your call?"

When she didn't answer, he put a hand on her shoulder. "I'd love to have dinner at the Kaines. With you." He squeezed her shoulder.

"But—"

"This is a way you can spend some time with them and not worry about the consequences. Tell Jennifer we'll come."

She stared at him, still uncertain.

"Whitney—" He stooped down beside her chair. "Trust me."

Whitney met his gaze. "I *do* trust you. But you can't stop Cory."

He got to his feet, then perched on the edge of the desk.

"You obviously don't know the reputation of the RUC."

"What?"

"Let's just say that there have been some ... ah ... accusations made about Northern Ireland's finest," he said with a grim smile. "Suffice it to say that they can be a rough bunch of lads if the occasion calls for it."

"I read the papers, Michael."

His eyes never left her face. "Then you must know that in all likelihood I'm not a very nice man."

Whitney put a hand on his arm, and he glanced at it. "I don't know what you used to be," she said. "And I don't think ... I care. I happen to think that you are ... a very nice man."

His gaze scanned her face for a moment. Finally, he broke the silence. "If you're to go on thinking I'm a good fellow, I'd best take a look at your plumbing problem." He motioned to the brown stain on the ceiling, which was still releasing a steady stream of water.

Whitney sighed. "It's probably a broken pipe."

He stood up. "I'll have a look. Perhaps I can patch it until you get someone in. It'll keep me out of your way until lunchtime."

"Lunchtime?"

"Yes, I thought we'd have lunch before facing the bear in his den. You are supposed to go out to see this Thomas Power, aren't you?"

"Michael, you don't have to go. I don't need a baby-sitter."

"Actually, it will give me a chance to shoot some landscape," he said, ignoring her attempted protest. "We'll take the Bronco. My equipment requires quite a lot of space."

"Michael, it's . . . several miles out—"

"More the better. I'm itching to get at these mountains. They're glorious." Resting his hands lightly on her shoulders, he grinned down at her. "Don't ever, *ever* argue with an Irishman, Whitney. We invented the art. Come on now, be a good lass and show me how to get upstairs."

Smiling, Whitney led him out into the hallway, stopping by the dark, narrow door that opened onto the stairs. "I hate it up there," she said, wrinkling her nose as she flipped the light switch.

At his questioning glance, she explained. "Mice," she said meaningfully.

"Ah, yes." He nodded with understanding, then tapped his inside left shoulder, saying, "Not to worry."

Puzzled, she frowned at him.

He stared down at her with a measured expression, then slowly parted his jacket to reveal a shoulder holster.

Whitney's entire body went cold. Her eyes went from the gun to his face.

"Sorry," he said tightly, closing his jacket.

"Why do you still carry a gun?" she asked quietly. "You're not a police officer anymore."

He looked at her, then touched the palm of his hand gently to her cheek. "But the bad guys are still out there, aren't they?"

Turning away from her, he started up the stairs.

Jennifer hung up the phone with a sigh. "So—how'd it go?" Daniel asked.

She turned to look at him. He was already at the piano this morning, propped comfortably in an enormous barrel-back chair with a stool shoved in front of him to elevate his leg. His computer was running, and he had a pot of fresh coffee on the stand to his right.

"She didn't say no."

"Did you tell her to ask Dev, too?"

"Oh, yes," Jennifer said dryly. "That's when she seemed to warm up to the idea."

He lifted his eyebrows but said nothing.

"She couldn't make lunch, though."

"Did she say why?"

"Yes, and I'm a little concerned." Jennifer walked over to the piano. "She's driving up to Blackwater Run this afternoon. To see Thomas Power."

Daniel frowned. "Who's responsible for that?"

"She didn't say, just that she'd had an urgent request from someone at Social Services." She paused. "I don't like the idea of Whitney going way out there by herself. That's a terrible road out to Holly Hill, and it gets even worse going up the mountain. Not to mention what kind of a reception she's likely to get from that—hermit."

"Tom Power is not a hermit," Daniel said mildly, giving the computer keyboard another couple of strokes and wincing at the weird sound that greeted his effort. "Wrong mode," he mumbled. "He's just a lonely, crippled old man who took a beating for half a century in the coal mines. Never married, never let anyone get close to him. No friends that I've ever heard about. He's had enough to make a man a little cranky."

"You know him?"

Daniel chuckled and shifted his weight in the chair. "He ran Gabe and me off his mountain a couple of times when we were teenagers. He was one mean rascal back then."

"Well, from what I've heard he hasn't mellowed any. I certainly hope he doesn't take his temper out on Whitney."

Again Daniel laughed softly. "You underestimate your little buddy. I think Whitney could turn back a swarm of mad bees if she set her mind to it. She's a lot sturdier than you think she is."

"I hope you're right." Jennifer watched him make a face at the next distorted cadence that wailed out of the speaker. "Whatever happened to that love song you were going to write?"

"I'm working on it," he answered testily.

"Define *love*."

His hand stopped, suspended above the keyboard, as he raised his head and sighed patiently.

"Kiss me good-bye, Jennifer."

"You want anything before I leave, Daniel?"

He nodded and went back to his keyboard. "A little respect, maybe."

SIXTEEN

THE Bronco lived up to its name, bucking to a stop after the roughest ride Whitney had ever experienced. As she closed her eyes and waited for her stomach to settle back into place, she silently promised herself that she would never ride a mountain road with Michael Devlin again.

Taking a close look at Thomas Power's residence, she couldn't help but wonder if the ride might not turn out to be the best part of the afternoon.

The place gave every appearance of being, in Michael's words, a "hermit's lair." Isolated against a densely wooded hillside, the small, unpainted cabin with its dusty windows and grim appearance seemed to shout a warning that visitors would not be welcome here.

As they got out of the car and approached the porch, however, Whitney took heart from the splash of fall flowers blooming all across the front of the cabin. Someone had gone to the trouble of adding some beauty and color to the otherwise dingy little home; she took that as a sign that the owner might not be as intimidating as she had heard.

Her hopes were dashed when two or three minutes of vigorous knocking produced no response.

She tried to call out as she knocked, but Michael gently gestured to her that her voice was too soft to be heard inside. He took over, pounding with a large fist while calling out Power's name.

When the door unexpectedly flew open, Whitney flinched and took a step backward, prepared for the worst. Standing straight, his shoulders braced in readiness, Michael watched the doorway with a look of frank curiosity.

The stooped, glowering man who appeared at the door wasn't what Whitney had expected. Not a big man, his height was dwarfed even more by his bent posture as he leaned heavily upon a walker.

Whitney's first sensation was one of genuine sympathy. *The poor, gray man,* she thought, smiling at him while he glared first at her, then at Michael. From head to toe, Thomas Power was colorless. His silver hair, looking uncombed but clean, topped an almost ashen face. Even the eyeglasses resting on his hawklike nose were rimmed with silver, the eyes behind them as cold as gunmetal. A worn charcoal cardigan hung open across a gray work shirt and darker gray pants.

Power lifted his lantern chin in obvious displeasure at this interruption.

Whitney recognized at once the need to tread carefully. "Mr. Power? I'm . . . Whitney Sharyn. From the Friend-to-Friend Association." Glancing at Michael, she went on. "And this is Michael Devlin. We'd like to visit with you for a few minutes if it's convenient."

Power pinned her in place with a belligerent, steely-eyed glare, giving no indication that he had heard her.

It occurred to Whitney that she really wasn't up to this, but she stood her ground, meeting the elderly man's stare with a level look of her own. "Could we come in, Mr. Power?"

"Why?"

The question surprised her, and Whitney fumbled for the right words. "Are you familiar with the . . . Friend-to-Friend Association, Mr. Power?"

He straightened an inch or so upward, and Whitney saw that his hands on the walker were white-knuckled, as if the slight movement had caused him intense pain. "No, I am not," he snarled with a menacing look. "Nor do I want to be."

Studying him, Whitney saw a man who was probably in his mid-seventies, a man severely crippled by arthritis. His right leg was bent inward as if it hadn't been straight for years. When he shifted on the walker, his arms appeared rigid and unbending. He was, she decided, a man who could use a helping hand, even if he resisted the idea. And she had little doubt that he *would* resist it.

Caution giving way to compassion, she met his gaze with a steady look. "I'd like to talk with you, Mr. Power. I think Friend-to-Friend could be of some . . . help to you, if you'll just let me . . . come in and explain—"

Her words seemed to stoke a blaze of resentment in him. His face contorted into an expression of pure nastiness as he lashed out at her. "I don't need your help! I don't want your help!" With the obvious intention of slamming the door in their faces, he started to turn away.

Whitney was unaware that Michael had spoken until she saw Thomas Power turn back and shoot the photographer a sharp, suspicious look.

She glanced up at Michael to read his lips and saw that his face was a mask of polite civility. "County Waterford, I should think? Lots of Powers in that area, aren't there?"

When Whitney looked back to Thomas Power, he was hunched, unmoving, his eyes narrowed suspiciously. Thrusting his head forward like a turtle, he gave the younger man a thorough, brutal appraisal. *"Who* thinks?"

Michael nodded coolly, stepped up closer to the door, and offered his hand. "Michael Devlin, sir."

Ignoring the younger man's hand, Power narrowed his eyes even more.

One of the lines that framed Michael's mouth deepened. Letting his hand drop to his side, he said simply, "Belfast."

The old man's face contorted. "Hah!" he sneered. "An Ulsterman!" He spat at Michael's feet, barely missing the toes of his hiking boots.

Whitney swiveled toward Michael, grabbing his arm in restraint.

He looked down at her, and she was amazed to see, not the fury she had expected, but a glint of amusement. He glanced down at his boots, then back to her, patting her hand as if to reassure her. Only then did he turn to Thomas Power.

With a brief shrug, he smiled cheerfully at the man. "Were you born here, Thomas Power, or did you come across?"

Power raked Michael's face with a fierce, measuring eye, his expression registering surprise at the younger man's aplomb. "Born on the Blackwater," he answered shortly. "Raised here."

Michael nodded and went on as smoothly as if he were carrying on a conversation with an old friend. "Live alone, do you, Thomas?"

Power's long, blade-edged mouth remained closed.

"I see. We passed a cabin on the way, just down the road from you. Thought it might be your place for a moment, but Miss Sharyn said it looked abandoned. Have you no neighbors at all, Thomas?"

The older man condescended to shake his head. "My brother's place. He's dead."

"I'm sorry."

"Don't be. We couldn't stand the sight of each other."

Michael put a fist to his mouth and dipped his head. When he lifted his face to again meet Power's gaze, his features were deceptively bland.

"Well, Thomas, Miss Sharyn here has put herself at great inconvenience to drop by. Do you think we could at least come in and talk a bit?"

Power combed the younger man's face with a scathing look of contempt before turning to Whitney. "She can," he finally said. "You can't."

Fascinated, Whitney watched Michael struggle to maintain his composure. It was obviously a battle, and she wouldn't have blamed him if he'd put the old man in his place.

Instead, he shifted his weight from one foot to the other, and with a slight lift of his chin said something that was wholly incomprehensible to Whitney.

Power's eyes sparked, then lost a fraction of their fire. His jaw, however, remained hard. "An Ulsterman speaking the Irish? I should think it would sour on your British tongue." He paused, then added, "I haven't heard it since my mam died, half my age ago. Never thought to hear it from a Brit."

Whitney watched Michael fight for control. The glint of amusement that had been in his eyes earlier faded. He said something else that Whitney assumed to be Gaelic, so strange were the shapes his lips formed.

When he had finished, Power stared at him, then pulled himself up into as straight a line as his crippled body could manage. He looked directly at Whitney. "I reckon the both of you can come in for a minute. But I don't have all day to chew the fat." Shooting another flinty look at Michael, he turned and, with obvious difficulty, shuffled back into the room.

"What in the world . . . did you say to him?" Whitney asked as they followed the old man inside.

Michael smiled down at her. "The only thing I could think of that might pierce his armor. I simply told him—in Gaelic—that his mother, God rest her soul, would be ashamed of his rudeness and his lack of hospitality." He paused, then explained. "We Irish, you see, pride ourselves on being a people of the open door. We tend to view hospitality not as a choice but as a way of life. I was counting on his remembering a few lessons learned at his mother's knee."

His eyes danced for a moment, and he leaned a little closer to her. "I also told him," he admitted, "that if he called me a 'Brit' one more time, I would see to it that the entire Social Services Agency showed up on his doorstep in the morning."

They entered through a Spartan kitchen—bare floor, wood table flanked by two chairs, and a small, fifties-vintage stove. The cabin was surprisingly neat—rustic and rudely furnished—but clean.

Power led them into what was obviously a combination bedroom and sitting room. Against the far wall was a bed with a sagging middle, covered by a thin white chenille throw. A kerosene heater sat in the middle of the floor, and facing it was a large platform rocker with a thin cushion. On the opposite wall squatted a faded, uncomfortable-looking plaid sofa.

There was no visible link to the outside world: no television set, no radio, no newspapers in sight. No frivolous souvenirs broke the austerity of the room; no family pictures gave it life or personality. The only hint that Thomas Power occasionally indulged in recreation was a small bookcase near the bed. Its shelves were crammed with a variety of books, all of which looked to be worn from use.

It was, Whitney thought with despair, the dwelling of a lonely, forgotten old man with a barren spirit.

They stayed for well over an hour, and in many ways, Whitney thought, it was one of the saddest hours she had ever spent. The more she learned about Thomas Power, the more she pitied him, although she was sure the very thought would have violated his precious independence.

He was far too proud for his own good. And it was the worst

kind of pride, Whitney knew—a pride that viewed any offer of help as an invasion of privacy.

Power had lived alone all these years, had never married, had apparently never allowed anyone to share his life, even after the mine accident responsible for crushing his leg. Whitney didn't miss how ill at ease he was—with her especially. At one point, she felt a sudden rush of sympathy for the old man. *Why, he's as awkward as a boy,* she realized. *It must make him miserably uncomfortable, having a woman in his cabin after all these years of being a bachelor.*

He had thawed a little by the time they rose to leave, but he wouldn't budge from his refusal to accept assistance. As they stood at the door preparing to leave, Whitney tried once more. "Mr. Power, it's not as if you'd be accepting charity."

He reddened. "You've got that right, miss. I've never taken a dime from no man, nor will I!"

"That's . . . what I'm trying to . . . explain to you," Whitney said. "It's entirely reciprocal—" She fumbled for a simpler word. "It's an *exchange* program, in a way. Someone helps you, and you help someone else. For example, I'm deaf, and—"

"Deaf?" Power leaned forward on his walker. "You can't hear?"

Whitney shook her head. "I read lips, Mr. Power. I can tell what you're saying . . . by watching you form your words."

He continued to study her. "I worked with a deaf-mute in the mines. He couldn't talk a lick. Talked on his hands, Uriah did." He stopped, then said grudgingly, "You talk pretty good for someone who can't hear."

It was, Whitney realized, the nicest thing Power had said to her since she had entered the cabin. She smiled at him with anticipation.

His next words, however, crushed her hopes that he might be softening. "Appreciate your coming all the way up here to talk to me. But I don't need none of what you're offering. It's not for me."

When Whitney started to speak, Michael touched her arm to stop her. She read his lips as he spoke. "Surely we can all use a bit of help from time to time, Thomas, don't you think?"

Whitney almost smiled at this, coming from Michael.

Power shot him a sour look. "This your woman?" he asked abruptly.

Michael glanced at Whitney, and for a moment something flared in his eyes that caused an uncomfortable stirring inside her.

"She's my friend," he finally replied. "And you'd do well to let her be yours, Thomas."

The two men locked gazes. Sensing the beginning of a duel, Whitney interrupted. "I'm sorry we . . . imposed, Mr. Power." She pulled a business card from her purse and handed it to him as she spoke. "We'll go now. But could I at least have someone . . . come by for you and bring you into town . . . for church on Sundays?"

He scowled. "I don't go to church."

"But if you'd like to—"

"I wouldn't," he said shortly. "I believe in the Almighty, mind you. But I'm of the thought that a body doesn't need to be sitting inside a cold vault on a hard pew in order to keep in touch with their Maker."

Frustrated, Whitney frowned at him. "But, Mr. Power, . . . don't you think God wants us to get to know each other? To worship together as a family? And to help one another?"

"Unlike some, miss," he replied with a twist of his mouth, "I don't pride myself on knowing the mind of the Creator."

Out of the corner of her eye, Whitney saw Michael lift one dark brow in evident exasperation. With a firm hand, he took her arm and turned her toward the steps. "If you change your mind, Thomas, you have Miss Sharyn's card." Not giving the old man time to reply, he propelled Whitney down the steps and back to the car.

Whitney glanced back over her shoulder to find that Thomas Power had already closed the door.

Michael's only comment as they pulled away from the cabin was a caustic remark about the old man's stubbornness. After that, he seemed to turn all his attention to the scenery around them, some of the most rugged, untamed terrain in the county.

For her part, Whitney was too disappointed in the outcome of the trip to care about making conversation. She had found herself drawn to Thomas Power in spite of his rudeness. She was convinced that he was more than just a fiercely independent, stiff-necked old man who wouldn't admit he needed anyone. He was elderly, crippled, rather frail, and most of all, lonely.

How did he handle the long mountain winters, she wondered, with his physical condition being what it was? Just getting himself in and out of a chair was an obvious effort. How did he get food? Medical supplies? She supposed some of the merchants in town delivered this far out, but what if there were an emergency? There was no way he could get off that mountain without help. Yet he apparently had no ties to the outside world, no family, no friends.

Lost in her anxious thoughts about the old man, she was surprised when Michael slowed the Bronco and bumped to a stop on the side of the road.

He turned to her and touched her shoulder. "Stop worrying about him," he said, leaning toward her. "There's nothing more you can do."

"Nobody should be . . . that alone."

"He chose his lifestyle, Whitney," Michael answered, not unkindly. "It wasn't forced on him."

Whitney studied his face. "Sometimes . . . it seems that way, I know. But I don't believe for a minute that Thomas Power is happy living . . . as he does. Circumstances created a pattern for him, and he . . . allowed it to happen. But don't try to convince me that he's happy, Michael. We both know he's not. He's a bitter, lonely old man without hope for anything better."

"And is that how you see me, Whitney? Unhappy, lonely—bitter?" His eyes searched her face.

Was he mocking her? Whitney was never sure with this man. He could turn from velvet to iron in a fraction of a second, making her head spin with confusion.

"Do you really want me to answer that, Michael?" she asked quietly.

"Why don't you?" He searched her eyes.

She met his gaze. "I . . . think you could easily end up that way, yes. Unless you allow yourself to need—and to be needed."

A muscle beside his eye jumped, and he turned away. As Whitney watched, his jaw tightened, then relaxed. When he faced her again, the warm light of affection had returned to his eyes. "And what if I should end up needing you, Whitney? What then?"

Yes . . . what then? Whitney asked herself, losing her breath at the look in his eyes.

Without warning, he did a lightning-fast mood shift. Tugging at her hand, he urged, "Come on—out! We're going to shoot some film. This is too grand to miss. Besides, I have to work every now and again, you know."

Laughing, Michael pulled her across the seat and out the door on his side, swinging her in the air for a moment before setting her down on the ground.

He retrieved his camera and binoculars from the back of the Bronco, handed Whitney the Leicas, then dropped the camera strap around his neck.

He took her hand, gesturing toward a breathtaking drop-off a few feet away to the right. "Let's go over there."

The air was much colder here than in the valley, sharp with the definite bite of late fall. Decaying leaves and moss made the ground spongy beneath their feet, and Whitney liked the way it felt as she walked. Breathing in the strong scent of pine and hard-wood, she began to relax a little for the first time since early morning.

While Michael started to frame and shoot his pictures, Whitney studied the valley below through the high-powered binoculars. She could see for miles. The mountains formed a wraparound palette of late-autumn colors: butterscotch and cinnamon-candy red, with random splashes of bronze and green. Hundreds of feet below, the entire valley was glazed in a shimmering, multicolored splendor.

Lowering the glasses, she gazed down at a wide shelf only a few feet below where they were standing. It extended outward several feet before dropping off to a deadly, seemingly bottomless fall. She took an instinctive step backward, satisfied to simply watch Michael work.

He had become a different person—an artist, with his camera a brush, the hills his canvas. Checking angles, adjusting for light, stooping and rising and pivoting back and forth, he was everywhere at once, moving with a fluid grace and a boyish exuberance that brought a smile to Whitney's face as she watched. She found it nearly impossible to reconcile this light-footed, energy-charged man in front of her with the other Michael Devlin—the man with the too-distant eyes and the too-hard mouth.

Finally he stopped moving and braced himself on the far edge of the roadside. Framed against a backdrop of rioting color, he hooded his eyes with his hand and stood gazing out over the sprawling valley. His face took on a look of infinite longing. Gone, at least for the moment, were the impassive stare, the stone mask, the impatient wariness. His eyes were yearning, his features vulnerable.

Abruptly he turned to smile at her. Whitney's heart skipped, setting off an alarm bell in her mind that she tried to ignore.

His face was flushed when he jogged over to her. "Let me take your picture. Please."

She started to shake her head, but he stopped her with the palm of his hand on her cheek. "Please," he said again. "I'll make only two prints: one for you, and one for me. I promise."

For a moment, Whitney almost wished he would revert to the other Michael, the one with the grim face and the hard eyes. That Michael was far easier to resist. This Michael was too winsome, too charming, too easy to care about.

"Humor me. I'll trade you a steak dinner for two pictures." He dipped his head, smiling into her eyes. "Well?"

Apparently, he could sense her weakening. He glanced around them, scanning the hill on the other side of the road. "Over there, against that patch of wildflowers. It's a perfect backdrop for you."

Whitney looked in the direction he was pointing, then turned back to him. His eyes pleaded, and she surrendered.

"Two prints, Michael," she reminded him sternly. "That's all."

He held up his hand in good faith. "Let me just get a different filter." He turned and headed for the car.

She watched him as he started back to her. He stopped for a moment to fuss with the lens on the camera, then gave her a smile and came to take her arm.

"The light's perfect," he said, guiding her across the road. "I'll get a great shot over here." As they reached the other side, he inclined his head toward a spot against the hillside. "Over there."

When she turned back to him, he was already focusing. "Yes, there. Can you still read my lips? All right, now lift your face a little. More. Look at me, Whitney." He made a quick adjustment. "Now, give me that wonderful smile. Ah, yes, that's it . . . just . . . like . . . that." He shot the picture, lowered the camera, and glanced around. "Let's go a bit farther down for the next one."

"I thought you were only going to take *one* picture."

"I can see you don't know all you should about photography. It can often take an entire roll of film to get that one perfect shot. And I'm afraid I am something of a perfectionist."

He grinned at her mutter of disgust.

Still grumbling, she let him take her arm and hurry her down the road a few more feet. "Here. Over here among these flowers."

His gaze swept their surroundings, then Whitney, his eyes going over her hair and her outfit with a nod of approval. He reached among the flowers growing along the bank and plucked a long stem of goldenrod. "You should always wear yellow," he said, smiling as he handed her the flower.

His expression sobered, and his hand lingered on hers for an instant longer than necessary. Whitney could see the conflict in his eyes as he continued to stare at her.

With one hand still holding hers, his other hand went to her shoulder. Gently, with great care, he pulled her into his arms, watching her, drawing her, at last holding her.

Losing her breath, Whitney felt herself falling—behind the mask, beyond the wall, into his heart. His lips touched her hair, then grazed her cheek. She had no idea whether she spoke his name aloud or simply thought it, but her mind began to hammer with the sound of it.

He drew back just enough so that she could see his face, read his lips. "Whitney . . . you shine, do you know that? Every place you go, everything you touch, you make it shine. Sometimes I almost believe that you could make my life shine, too."

He framed her face with both hands. "Can you see yourself shining in my eyes, Whitney? Can you?"

She tried to speak his name, but the word on her lips was voiceless. He touched the corner of her mouth, then pressed his lips to the place he had touched. Pulling back only a whisper's distance, his eyes questioned hers, then made the decision for both of them.

His kiss was tender, infinitely gentle, little more than a brief, fleeting touch. He released her slowly, with obvious reluctance. She felt his hands, the hands that always looked so large and powerful and confident, tremble on her shoulders as he stepped back from her.

They stood that way for a suspended moment, his eyes caressing her face, his expression both tender and uncertain.

"I care for you deeply, Whitney," he finally said. "I have no right to feel this way for you, but I do."

"No right?" Whitney felt stunned, dazed by the depth of feeling she could read in his eyes.

"You're so—good. I'm almost afraid I'll taint you with my touch."

Dismayed, Whitney put her hand to his lips to silence him. "Don't."

"Whitney, you don't know me."

She smiled as she studied the lines of his face. "I think I know the man you are. But you're still . . . running from the man you used to be."

His eyes were troubled, his mouth tight. "They're the same."

Whitney shook her head. "No, I don't think so. I think I know the . . . real Michael."

An expression flitted across his face—almost, she thought, a look of . . . fear.

"There are things I have to tell you, Whitney. You won't feel the same about me when you know."

She sighed. "Michael, I've read . . . about Belfast. I've seen the films . . . on television. I know about . . . some of the things your police force has been accused of doing."

He paled, and once more she touched his cheek. "That's why you resigned, isn't it? That's why you left and came to the United States? Because you couldn't stand being a part of all that."

"That's true, yes. But it's not that simple, Whitney. That's not all of it—"

"The only thing I need to know is that you gave it up. That part of your life is over, Michael."

He closed his eyes, tight, then opened them. "There's more." As she watched, his face once again underwent a transformation, shifting back to a look of strained control. "We'll talk tonight. There's a great deal I need to tell you. Much of it I should have told you before now, but I was waiting for—the right time."

Puzzled, Whitney put her hand on his arm. "Michael?"

"Later. Not here. Come on, now, let me get this shot before we lose the light. The sun's already slipping."

He took two more shots, his demeanor reverting to professional detachment. "Almost done. Let me have one more, right down there, close to that boulder."

Her pulse still racing and the goldenrod still in her hand, Whitney turned and started walking. The road was steep, almost straight down. A patchwork quilt of dozens of different kinds of wildflowers checkered the hillside.

She stopped beside the boulder, waited until he focused her in the viewfinder and took a few more shots.

When Michael turned aside and began fiddling with his camera, Whitney studied him. What had transpired between them, and why? She wasn't sure. She knew only that she was badly shaken, and confused.

A few yards to her right she spied the abandoned cabin they had seen on the way up, the cabin that had belonged to Thomas Power's brother. It rested deep inside a thicket, surrounded by overgrown brush and shrubs. The windows were filthy, the siding unpainted. And yet it drew her—the isolation of it, the loneliness. Curiosity stirred in her, and Whitney moved closer.

Tire tracks ran parallel with the right side of the cabin. She followed them until they veered off into a small glade that immediately narrowed and disappeared into the woods.

When Whitney reached the porch, she stopped and examined

the steps to make sure they looked safe. Satisfied, she took the half-dozen steps slowly and carefully, going to the front window to look in.

The pane was covered with dust and grime, but she thought she could make out the lines of a few pieces of furniture inside. She moved as close as she could to the window without actually pressing her face against the dirty glass. The interior was dim and shadowed, but she could see a table and what appeared to be a sagging couch.

Another window at the opposite end of the porch beckoned to her, and she started toward it. This one was smaller and more narrow. Cupping her hands at her temples to block the light, she squinted through the dusty glass.

She was looking into a bedroom. An old iron bed, covered with a blanket, was directly across from her. A chair sat beside it. She moved in still closer, smudging her face on the windowpane in order to get a better look. Frowning, she saw what appeared to be clothing laid out across the middle of the bed.

Whitney's mind told her she was imagining it, that she couldn't possibly be seeing what she thought she was seeing. Heedless now of the dirty windowpane, she pushed her face against the glass and stared into the room.

Her eyes widened with growing horror, and the goldenrod fell from her hand. She wasn't mistaken. She wasn't imagining it. The clothing on the bed was a neatly arranged, black-and-white Pierrot costume.

SEVENTEEN

I T was incredible luck. Unbelievable. He couldn't have planned it any better. After all those months of scheming, acting, making himself out to be a rehab so those brain-dead doctors would let him out, it was finally over.

Even after he had found her, it had taken another two weeks to come up with this place. He had sensed all along that the success of the entire production might depend on staying out of sight, undiscovered, until he was ready to make his final appearance. The cabin was like a gift: close enough to town so he could come and go at will, far enough from people and traffic so he needn't worry about interference.

But to have her *delivered* to him like this, to have her just walk up on the porch as if she were coming for a visit—it blew him away. He had thought all along he would have to take her by force, grab her from her apartment or somewhere else.

It had been a wild shot, calling her office yesterday with a message for her to visit old man Power. He had counted on her inability to say no to someone who needed help, and he thought the old duck up the road might be just enough to lure her up here. Even so, he'd thought he would have to force her off the road.

Instead, she was standing at the door, practically begging to come in.

Little Red Riding Hood—meet the big bad wolf. . . .

He clamped his teeth down on his bottom lip to keep from laughing out loud.

With his stomach pressed close to the ground, he inched forward a little more, moving just close enough to the edge of the rise to get a clear view of the man below.

The boyfriend. He hadn't counted on him being along. He had wanted her alone, in her car. His hand caressed the gun at his side, then tightened on the butt as he stared down at the road. No matter. He'd take care of him, then her. *Two for one . . . both for me.*

Yeah, all the luck was swinging his way now. The proof was right in front of him. Right down there on the road. The guy was just standing there, tinkering with the camera. An open target.

He couldn't see Whitney from here, but it didn't matter. She would still be there, right where she was when he had come across the back of the hill. Standing on the porch, peering through the cabin windows.

He had almost missed them. He had kept an eye on the road all day, finally going inside long enough to get something to eat. The sound of a car engine had sent him back to the door to look outside. Sure enough, the Bronco had pulled off, just up the hill.

Now he wouldn't have to make another trip into town. If she hadn't shown up on the hill today, he had planned to go back into town again tonight and hide in that upstairs storeroom while she was at her weekly prayer meeting. Later, he could grab her and bring her out here to the cabin. He was tired of waiting. This part of the play was losing its appeal.

But the waiting was over. She had come to him. He didn't have to do a thing but get rid of the jerk she was with and go down to the cabin to meet her.

The whole scenario was perfect. Beautiful.

He scooted up another inch, looking down at the dark head

almost directly below him. The guy was wide open. He could blow his head apart from up here.

He smothered another laugh. Poor little Whitney wouldn't even know what had happened. Down there at the cabin, she was too far off the road to see anything. He grinned. And for sure, she wouldn't *hear* anything.

By the time she realized her boyfriend had been wasted, it would be too late. She'd be where she belonged by then. Inside the cabin, with him.

His blood began to boil as he remembered all the months he had lost because of her, the humiliation he'd suffered because of her. Everything that had gone wrong had been her fault. Stringing him along the way she had, pretending to be his woman all those weeks, and then trying to drop him cold at the end. Because of her, he had lost his job, lost his standing with the players club—and just about lost his mind cooped up in that nuthouse all those months.

She owed him, all right. She owed him plenty. And he didn't intend to wait any longer to collect.

He pushed off his stomach and got to his knees, hugging the gun to his side. Then he stood up, planted his feet, and aimed the .38.

The dark-haired man on the road below still had his head bent, studying the camera in his hands.

Suddenly, as if sensing movement above him, his head shot up, and his hand slid inside the field jacket.

At the exact moment Ross squeezed off his first shot, the guy on the road feinted left, firing as he pivoted to a crouch.

Ross started moving as soon as he saw the boyfriend go for his gun. Hitting the ground, he twisted and rolled behind a bush. Their bullets whistled and sliced the air as they crossed.

The boyfriend jumped for cover behind a boulder near the road, but Ross got off another shot before he landed, and this one hit its target. The guy went down, slamming his head against a boulder as he fell.

Ross waited, then scrambled down the side of the hill. The guy was sprawled in the middle of the road. He flipped him over with the toe of his boot.

A narrow ribbon of blood trickled from his hairline, just above his ear. He was unconscious, but alive.

The shot had only nicked him. Probably the blow from the fall had done more damage. He aimed his gun to finish him, then lowered it again.

He'd take him back to the cabin first. Whitney and this guy had seemed to have something going. It might be more interesting if he brought the boyfriend along. Every play should have an audience, after all. Sure. He'd keep him around for a while, then finish him off later, when it was time to take Whitney and get out.

Watching him, Ross stooped down and picked up the revolver that had been knocked loose by the fall. He pocketed the gun, then ripped the strap off the camera and used it to bind the other's hands behind his back.

He straightened, studying the unconscious man. He could probably carry him; they were about the same size, except this guy was leaner. He decided against it. Shifting his gun to the other hand, he slipped his right arm under the man's bound hands, turned, and started to drag him down the road as if he were nothing but a large, cumbersome bag of laundry.

As soon as he turned, he saw her. She was standing in the middle of the road, staring up at him, wild-eyed with fear. She whirled around, apparently about to run in the opposite direction. Then, abruptly, she turned back as if she had only then realized what Ross was dragging behind him.

When she started to run toward him, screaming at him as she came, Ross smiled and waved his hand—the hand holding the gun—in greeting.

EIGHTEEN

JENNIFER glanced at the clock on the dash as she passed the city limits sign. Almost three-thirty. She had promised Daniel she would be back in town before five.

He had given her a hard time when she called him from the station to tell him where she would be. Not that she would have expected anything else. He liked to pretend that he didn't worry about her, that he respected her independence—but he worried, all right. *And I wouldn't have it any other way,* she admitted with a smile.

Even after she had explained that it would be easier for her to make a run up to Power's cabin and check on Whitney than to spend the afternoon worrying, the teasing edge had remained in his voice.

"Jennifer, Whitney is a grown woman—a mature, professional, extremely competent woman. She drives anywhere she wants to go. Alone. You don't have to tailgate her."

"I'm not concerned about her *driving,* Daniel. That's not why I'm going."

"Then why *are* you going?"

When she fumbled for the words to make him understand, Jennifer realized that *she* didn't quite understand. She thought her uneasiness had as much to do with the peculiar way Whit-

163

ney had been acting as with the treacherous road and Thomas Power's formidable reputation.

Making a right onto Holly Hill, she turned on the radio to get the station's three-thirty news. Lee Kelsey was already into his report. Jennifer made a mental note to be sure his pay reflected all the overtime hours he had been putting in lately.

"Law enforcement officials in Kentucky and surrounding states are on the lookout for a former mental patient released several weeks ago from a Kentucky facility for the criminally insane. Cory Ross, committed to the institution a little over a year ago after the brutal beating of a young deaf teacher in Louisville, was released on a probationary basis subject to a number of conditions. . . ."

Jennifer's heart lurched, then began to race. She reached to turn up the volume, slowing the car for the stop sign just ahead at Blackwater Run.

". . . Ross, now believed to be a suspect in at least three, possibly more, brutal slayings of young women in Kentucky, Indiana, and Ohio, failed to comply with the terms of his release by not appearing for his first out-patient counseling session. In addition, Ross is wanted for questioning in a number of random assaults on both male and female victims along the Kentucky–West Virginia border. . . ."

Jennifer's hands were shaking so violently on the wheel that she could hardly keep the car under control. She knew she was losing part of the broadcast, knew she should be getting every detail, that it was important, but her mind insisted on isolating and replaying only a part of it over and over again. *". . . a little over a year ago after the brutal beating of a young deaf teacher in Louisville. . . ."*

Halfway up the hill, the car choked and rebelled against the steep grade. Downshifting, she tightened her grip on the wheel. The hill was straight up, the road narrow and potholed. The tension in her shoulders grew, matching the tight clench of dread around her heart. With an effort, she forced her attention back to Lee's voice.

"*. . . The following description has been issued by the Kentucky State Police. Ross is thirty years old; approximately five-foot eleven, one hundred eighty-five pounds; dark blond hair; brown eyes; clean shaven. . . .*"

Her eyes went to the forlorn little cabin on the right, and she slowed. She had thought Thomas Power's place was farther up the hill, and there was no sign of Whitney's car. Still, there weren't that many cabins up here; she'd better stop and check. It could be that Whitney had already been here and gone, but she wanted to be sure.

When she spotted the Bronco several feet up on the other side of the road, she looked at it blankly for an instant. *Devlin's car!* What was *he* doing up here? Where was Whitney?

Her pulse hammering, she twisted the wheel and jolted off the road, letting the engine idle in park. She sat unmoving, her hands still locked on the steering wheel as she stared at the small, unpainted cabin half hidden in the thicket. There was no sign of life.

"*. . . It is believed that Ross often relies on theater costumes for disguise. One assault victim, who has tentatively identified Ross as her assailant, stated that he was wearing a black-and-white clown suit during the attack. . . .*"

Jennifer turned off the engine, yanked her keys from the ignition, and jumped out of the car.

Daniel's hand shook as he set his half-full cup of coffee down on the kitchen countertop. Digging into the floor with his crutch, he hobbled to a stool, his attention still riveted on Lee's voice.

"*. . . State police warn that Ross is probably armed and should be considered extremely dangerous. If you have any information regarding the suspect, please notify your local law-enforcement agency immediately.*"

Shaken, his mind went into reverse, first locking on Whitney's attack the night of the festival, then coming to rest on Jennifer's concern about her friend's "odd behavior"—her withdrawal, her evasion.

With the help of the crutch, he pushed himself off the stool and went to the wall phone by the refrigerator.

Pushing the first memory button, the one programmed for the police, he waited. As soon as the dispatcher answered, he asked for Rick Hill.

He leaned heavily on the crutch, drumming the fingers of his free hand against the nearby countertop. As soon as the young officer answered the phone, Daniel started talking.

Hill knew Whitney's description of her assailant. He also knew about the interstate APB. In fact, as Daniel related Jennifer's concern about the "recent change" in Whitney, he began to get a sense that the policeman might know even more.

Abruptly, he stopped. "The man in the Pierrot suit—the one who attacked Whitney at the festival—it was Ross, wasn't it? And she was the 'young deaf teacher' he attacked in Louisville." When Hill didn't answer right away, he pressed. "Rick?"

Daniel heard throat-clearing at the other end of the line. Then, "Dan . . . without breaking a certain confidence, I can't give you any details about how I got my information, but—yes. Miss Sharyn was the teacher in Louisville." There was a long sigh. "And if she *has* seemed—different—lately, she's had plenty of cause for it."

The anxiety that had begun to creep over Daniel at the beginning of the news broadcast hit full force. "Rick," he interrupted shortly, "how about sending a patrol car out here?"

"What?"

Quickly, Daniel explained about Whitney's trip out to Thomas Power's place and Jennifer's insistence on following her. "I don't have any real reason for thinking they might be in trouble, but if

Whitney *is* in jeopardy in any way, then my wife is, too—because she's on the way out there. Rick, would you come and get me? As soon as possible."

"Dan, I'll take another man with me and go check—"

"I don't care how many men you take, Rick, so long as you take me, too." He paused. "Please."

Not waiting for an answer, he hung up and then called his mother to see if she could meet Jason's bus.

NINETEEN

A LATE-AFTERNOON gloom surrounded the house. The thicket held a suffocating depth of silence. Jennifer could hear her pulse hammering in her ears as she climbed the steps to the dilapidated cabin.

Just outside the door, she stopped to listen.

What she heard drove a blade of terror straight through her heart.

Whitney, weeping. And a man's voice, rough and impatient.

Jennifer edged a little closer to the door, close enough that the side of her face pressed against the splintering wood.

The man's voice suddenly quieted. But Whitney went on sobbing.

The sound wrenched Jennifer's heart. Unable to think beyond the moment, she twisted the doorknob with a trembling hand.

Without warning, the door exploded inward, hurtling her into the midst of a nightmare.

An iron-muscled arm swathed in black silk went around her throat, choking off her breath. Jennifer tried to scream, but the arm tightened even more against her windpipe. The sound that escaped was little more than a pitiful mew.

"Shut up!" The man's voice was heavy and coarse with rage.

Whitney was sitting on a chair in the middle of the room at a square, battered table. Her hands were handcuffed behind her, her arms shackled to the chair. On the table in front of her was an open makeup kit, beside it a mirror on a swivel base.

For one awful moment, she met Jennifer's gaze. Her lovely, enormous eyes were now sunken pools of terror in a white mask. The perfect features had been painted with clown white. The delicate mouth was a grotesque red slash. Black paint from the weeping eyes tracked dark paths all the way down both sides of her face.

Jennifer's throat swelled with anguish. She cried out and tried to lunge forward, but a calloused hand smeared with white makeup went over her mouth, and she was shoved, hard, onto a chair at Whitney's right.

Stunned, she saw Michael Devlin slumped in a chair at the opposite end of the table, his head lolling weakly forward, his hands bound with rope behind him. A ribbon of blood furrowed the left side of his face, and an ugly bruise darkened his temple on the right. His eyes were open but not fully focused. The collar of his field jacket was stained with blood. On the table in front of him were his keys, his wallet, and what remained of his camera.

Jennifer made herself look up at the man standing beside her with a gun pointed at her head.

"Don't move, chick. Don't even breathe."

He wasn't overly tall, but in spite of the billowing Pierrot costume, Jennifer could tell that he was heavily muscled. His cold, obsidian eyes conveyed a brutal kind of power. His face was covered in clown white—like Whitney's—with the same exaggerated red mouth and black paint accenting his eyes.

Jennifer's heart pounded painfully against her rib cage as she stared with revulsion into the malevolent, painted face.

"I suppose you just happened to be in the neighborhood," he sneered.

Jennifer twisted on the chair, and he rammed the gun against the side of her head. "Don't—move, I said."

After an excruciatingly long moment, he pulled the gun back an inch or so. "Where's the hulk?"

"Wh-what?" Jennifer blinked, swallowing hard.

"Your old man. The blind boy."

Anger flared, but Jennifer fought the urge to fly at him.

"Laid up, is he?"

Something in his voice made Jennifer look up at him. His expression was amused, gloating.

In that instant, she knew who he was. The truth came rushing in on her like an icy wall of floodwater, and she realized everything at once: this was Cory Ross, the escapee she had heard about on the news. He was the animal responsible for Daniel's broken leg.

And Whitney was the "young deaf teacher" he had brutalized in Louisville.

Shaking as much from anger as from fear, she watched Ross reach across the table for a length of rope. He turned and, tucking the gun under his arm, bound Jennifer's hands to the chair behind her.

He straightened, pulled the gun from beneath his arm, and leveled it once more at her head.

"The blind man know where you are?" he asked abruptly.

Unable to speak, Jennifer simply stared at the dark opening of the gun barrel.

With a mocking smile, Ross touched the cold tip of the gun barrel to her temple. Jennifer shuddered, her breath coming in gasps.

"Doesn't matter," he muttered, finally breaking the silence. "The blind man doesn't worry me."

He lowered the gun and walked across the room to a sagging couch, where he placed the .38 beside another revolver.

As he came back to the table, he directed his words to Jennifer.

"Well, since you're here, I suppose we'll have to find a part for you."

"What?" Jennifer looked at him numbly. She felt the first cold tremors of shock setting in. She shook her head to clear it, determined not to allow this maniac to intimidate her.

With the same calculating smile, he glanced from her to Whitney. "A part, babe. A part in my play. Whitney and I have the leads, so you and the cameraman here will have to settle for supporting roles." He turned back to Jennifer then, and as she stared up into his hideously made-up countenance, she felt as if she had just come face-to-face with evil itself.

Unexpectedly, Ross whirled around to Devlin, appraising the wounded photographer with hard eyes.

"Something bothers me about you, cameraman," he said, his eyes never leaving the journalist's face as he began to yank bills and cards from Devlin's wallet, tossing them randomly onto the table. "I'm trying to figure out why you'd pack a .357 Magnum with your camera. Why don't you explain that to me?"

He glanced down at the billfold, frowning as he pried something out of the concealed bill compartment. For a moment he stood staring at the laminated card in his hand. When he looked up, his eyes burned with rage.

He slapped the card down on the table, then snaked an arm out and grabbed the journalist by his hair, yanking his head back hard enough to make Jennifer wince.

Devlin cried out, and his face turned ashen.

"Cory—don't!"

At Whitney's outburst, Ross turned to her without releasing his grip on Devlin. "Shut up!"

Picking the card up off the table, he waved it in front of Devlin. "Where's your shield, cop?" he snarled.

He leaned down to Devlin's level, still holding him by the hair. *"Cop!"* He made the word an obscenity.

He released Devlin's hair and shoved his hand into the photographer's bloodstained field jacket, patting down the lining. When he freed his hand from the coat, he was holding a badge.

Ross glanced from the ID card to the badge, then flung them onto the table.

"I *knew* you had a stink on you!" he shouted. "I was smelling *cop!*"

Her eyes shifting wildly between the two men, Whitney again cried out. "Cory, no! He's not a policeman anymore! He's—"

"A *detective!* A *Cincinnati detective!*" Ross hissed furiously. He grasped Devlin by the back of the neck, slamming him facedown on the table hard enough to lift the chair off the floor as it pitched forward.

Devlin groaned, and Ross again snapped his head back by the hair. "What's your name, cop? What are you doing here? And don't tell me you're *moonlighting!*"

Devlin's eyes went to Whitney, who was staring at him with wounded disbelief. "Michael?"

His eyes pleaded with her as he shook his head miserably. "I was going to tell you, Whitney. I was going to tell you tonight—"

"Then it's true?" she interrupted him. "You're . . . a detective?"

Nodding, he continued to entreat her with his eyes.

Whitney stared at him, her expression hurt and confused.

Jennifer didn't understand what was happening. A part of her wanted to strike out at Devlin for his deceit, for bringing that terrible look of pain to Whitney's eyes. Yet at the same time she felt sympathy for the man, for the abuse he was suffering at Ross's hands.

"Why did you . . . lie to me?" Whitney's question was an indictment.

"I didn't—exactly lie, Whitney—"

"You *lied,* Michael!" Her words sounded as if she were strangling.

He shook his head in defeat.

"What was I, Michael?" Whitney went on in a choked voice. "Your . . . *bait?*" Her eyes raked his face accusingly.

He looked at her. "No! It wasn't like that, I meant to *protect* you—"

Tears coursed down Whitney's cheeks, smearing the clown white into a pathetic visage.

He looked away from her, saying nothing.

Ross, who had been listening to the exchange in contemptuous silence, broke in. "This is good material, but I'm afraid we'll have to trash it for now." Bracing both hands on the table, he eyed the detective. "Let's just cut to the chase, all right? What, exactly, is *Detective* Michael Tierney from Cincinnati doing in Shepherd Valley, West Virginia?"

Jennifer frowned as both she and Whitney, almost in unison, repeated, *"Tierney?"*

Ross looked from one woman to the other, his eyes narrowing.

Michael's gaze was fixed on Whitney. "My last name is Tierney. Devlin is my middle name."

"Where are you from, anyway?" Ross snapped. "You're not American. How can you be a cop when you're not even an American?"

"I'm from Northern Ireland," the detective answered shortly. "But I'm an American citizen."

"I'm an American citizen," Ross mimicked. "Why don't you learn to talk like one, then, cop?" He moved a little closer to Michael. "You're here because of me, right?"

Michael lifted his face and shot a scathing look of contempt at Ross but said nothing.

"Talk to me, Irish. I asked you a question."

The detective hesitated. Jennifer felt some terrible kind of anger emanating from him, but as she watched, he seemed to gain control and subdue it.

When he finally answered Ross, his voice was even. "I'm part of an interstate investigation."

"And what, exactly, are you investigating, Irish?" The white makeup made Ross's eyes look as dark—and hard—as chunks of coal.

When Devlin didn't respond, Ross's hand again whipped out and seized his hair. "I said *talk,* cop!"

Michael grimaced at the pain but remained silent.

With an abrupt shake of his head, Ross released him. "Never mind. We both know what you're investigating, don't we, Irish?"

Devlin's reply was a hard stare.

"Yeah, we know." Ross said with a shrug. "Doesn't matter anyway. You're history."

He turned his back on the detective and came to stand beside Jennifer.

She shrank inwardly, steeling herself not to move when she felt his eyes on her, even though the thought of him touching her made her skin crawl.

To her surprise, he began to untie her hands.

"Don't get excited, chick," he said with a dry laugh as he freed her from the chair. "This is only temporary. You're coming with me for a minute."

Jennifer felt the blood drain from her face. "Wh-where are you taking me?"

"Hey!" He turned on her, his face a ghastly white mask. "This is *my* play! You don't ask the questions—*I* do."

Jennifer's gaze went to Michael, who gave her a small shake of his head and a look of warning.

"Get up!" Ross yelled at her, reaching across the table for Michael's keys.

Jennifer started to rise, but her legs went weak, and she nearly buckled. She grasped the edge of the table to steady herself.

Ross jerked her arm behind her and started hauling her backward across the floor. Reaching the couch, he bent sideways to pick up one of the guns.

"We're going to get rid of her car and the Bronco," he said, his breath hot and sour at the side of Jennifer's face. "And you two are going to stay right where you are until we get back."

His voice was thick with menace. "If either one of you moves an inch away from that table, I'll blow your snoopy little friend here all over the mountain. This will only take a couple of minutes, Whitney-love. When I come back, you can put on your costume, and we'll do a little rehearsing. Irish and your buddy here can be our audience."

Whitney's eyes filled with raw terror.

Ross tightened his grip on Jennifer, pocketing his own gun before picking up the Magnum and pressing the tip of its barrel against Jennifer's cheek. "Don't worry, chick. Irish will do as he's told. He knows exactly what his .357 will do to a pretty lady's head, don't you, cop?"

With his free hand he flung the door open and backed out onto the porch. "Where's your keys?"

"M-my jacket pocket," Jennifer stammered, reaching with her left hand to pull them out. At her movement he gave an oath and wrenched her arm even harder. Jennifer cried out against the pain.

"I'll tear it off if you don't shut your mouth!" he warned her.

When they reached the bottom step, he released her, giving her a push toward the Honda. "We'll pull it back there in the woods with mine," he said, motioning to a dense grove of trees behind the cabin.

Ross shoved her behind the steering wheel, then ran around to get in on the passenger's side, leveling the gun at her as soon as he hit the seat.

Jennifer's mind began to race. Somehow she had to get away from him and go for help. But the man had two guns and probably outweighed her by half. Tears of helplessness stung her eyes as she put the key in the ignition. There was nothing she could do. Nothing. At least not yet.

"Don't try anything cute," he said, smiling at her through the bloodred slash that framed his mouth. "You might want to keep in mind that you're the most expendable member of this troupe."

Whitney could feel Michael's eyes on her after Cory dragged Jennifer from the room. She saw him dip his head toward her, knew he was trying to get her to look at him. But she wouldn't. She couldn't bear the pain.

Somehow she knew that the anguish she was feeling at this moment was much worse than any physical punishment Cory would eventually inflict on her. She had never known that betrayal could be such a consuming, annihilating agony.

Out of the corner of her eye, Whitney saw him twist on the chair, and she knew he was willing her to turn and look at him.

And, finally, she did.

The urgency in his eyes caught and held her. "I know you're angry and hurt," he said. He slowed his words a little so she could read his lips more easily. "And you have a right. But I need you to understand why I did what I did. Whitney, don't you see? I was afraid that if you knew too much, it would go worse for you if Ross found you. That he'd think you had—conspired with me. Whitney—don't look away from me. Please."

Blood ran down one side of his face. An angry bruise marked the other side. Whitney wanted to touch the bruise, clean away the blood. She wanted to heal him. She wanted to hit him.

"Whitney? Remember, I told you that we'd talk tonight. I was going to tell you everything—and then find somewhere else for you to stay."

At her puzzled frown, he explained. "When I went upstairs to the storeroom today—to see about the leak—I found that Ross had been up there."

Whitney averted her eyes. *Don't think about it. Don't think about Cory being upstairs, in the same house . . . waiting.*

She didn't have to think about it. Hadn't she sensed it, or at least sensed the threat of his presence?

She looked at Michael, realized he was waiting to get her attention again. "Someone had been scratching or carving on the floor, probably with a pocketknife," he told her. "Killing time, I expect. Like some people scribble on a sheet of paper." He paused, hunching a shoulder as if to ease its stiffness. "I knew I couldn't let you spend another night in that house. I would have told you the truth tonight—everything. I intended to take you somewhere then, somewhere safe, where you would have round-the-clock protection until we locked Ross up again.

"Whitney, when this is over—don't look at me like that, it *will* be over, I promise you—I'll explain everything. There's no time now. I want you to do exactly what Ross tells you. I know you're frightened, but I believe you can keep yourself alive by going along with him. Whitney . . . he's killed three women that we're sure of, perhaps others. Assaulted and beaten even more, most likely."

Whitney's stomach knotted. Michael pulled in a deep breath and continued. "He's mad, Whitney. Completely insane. You already know that. His mind is hanging by only the weakest of threads. If you defy him, he could explode. This is all a play to him—an obscene, mad play. You must pretend to play your part. Do exactly what he tells you to do. Don't cross him. Don't anger him. Don't even question him. Just—go along with him."

Whitney shook her head hopelessly. "It won't . . . help. He's going to kill me. . . ."

"No!" Michael's eyes blazed. "You can buy time for yourself—for all of us! And time is what we need, Whitney."

"You don't know him, you . . ."

Michael's face changed, tightening to a stony mask that made Whitney catch her breath. "I know him. I know him all too well. I know what he's done . . . to his victims. I know the extent of his depravity. I've lived with his madness, studied it, for over a year now, just so I could trap him and put him away for good."

"And you used me," Whitney accused him, "for *bait!* You lied to me."

He shook his head. "No, not entirely. I *am* a photojournalist—at least part-time. It was merely a hobby at first. My way of dealing with the stress of the job. Then a couple of years ago some of my stuff was published. I've been selling to the nationals fairly regularly ever since."

"But you came here because you thought I'd lead you to Cory?" she persisted.

He hesitated. "I suspected he would try to find you, yes. And by then, I had almost become obsessed with putting him behind bars for the rest of his natural life. One of his victims was a young girl, a student at the University of Cincinnati." His features were taut as he continued. "She was my partner's niece. I saw what Ross did to her—he beat her to death—and I couldn't forget it. I began to study the sheets, looking for the same MO. And I finally found the lead I was looking for in two other fatal assaults, one in Louisville, another in Indiana. I started building a file and working with an interstate team. When I learned about Ross being institutionalized after your beating, I spent several days in Louisville. By the time I left, I was convinced I'd found my man."

His mouth thinned. "My every instinct told me Ross was the one we were looking for. But I had to prove it. I kept on with the investigation in my spare time, all those months he was in the asylum. When they released him, I asked for a leave. I wanted to build an absolutely airtight case against him. By then I felt certain he'd go after you again." He paused, his expression turning even harder. "It seems that Ross doesn't handle rejection very well."

Whitney nodded. She had been afraid, even knowing Cory was confined, that eventually he would look for her. "How . . . did you find me?"

He shrugged. "It's never that hard, not for the police. Most people have no idea how many loose ends they leave behind when they try to disappear. Once I found you, I figured it was just a matter of time before Ross showed up."

"So you *were* . . . using me," Whitney accused him.

Michael's eyes searched hers for a moment before he answered. "In a way. But I was also trying to save your life." He swallowed, then added, "And perhaps mine."

At her puzzled look, his features softened, and he managed a faint smile. "Read my lips, Whitney. If I don't have the chance to tell you anything else, I want you to know this much. It isn't the way I'd have chosen to tell you, but it's the truth, nevertheless."

As he spoke, his face, haggard and pain-shadowed, began to relax, just a little.

"The first time I looked at your picture," he said, "I saw something in your eyes. I had no idea what it was, only that it was something I had to find. As mad as it sounds, I saw something looking out at me from your eyes that was almost like a touch of healing. I began to think that if I could find you, I might find—" He stopped, shaking his head uncertainly. "I don't know what, exactly." He looked at her. "Hope, perhaps. Healing. I'm not sure."

Whitney searched his eyes.

"I didn't understand it either," he said. "It almost frightened me. I only knew that I couldn't live with myself unless I found you and tried to give you your freedom from Ross. I know now that I was counting on gaining my own freedom as well."

A raw ache had begun to gnaw at Whitney's heart. She wanted to believe him. . . . oh, how she wanted to believe.

180

"Whitney . . . I can't touch you, but look at my eyes. A man should touch a woman when he tells her he loves her. My eyes are touching you, Whitney. I love you. I think I've loved you since the first time I held your photograph and looked into those incredible eyes of yours. I love you, and I . . . need you. I think . . . if you'll allow me to love you . . . and if you can love me back, perhaps in time I can learn to love others as well. The way you love. Whitney, if you don't believe anything else, believe that."

In that instant, Whitney *did* believe him. And she wanted more than anything else in the world to give him the healing, the hope, he so desperately needed.

Whitney closed her eyes, fighting back the tears. The kind of healing Michael needed was beyond her, no matter how much she loved him. And she *did* love him. But only God could give Michael what he needed. Only God.

And so in that moment she prayed that, whatever happened to her in the following hours, God would protect . . . and heal . . . Michael. *Heal his heart, Lord . . . his lonely, searching heart.*

She opened her eyes then. "I . . . do believe you, Michael. I . . . trust you."

They were still holding each other close with their eyes when the door flew open.

Ross came barreling through it, waving his gun, shoving Jennifer across the room with a force that sent her flying against the table. He was shaking with anger, screaming something too fast and too wild for Whitney to catch.

It was Michael who mouthed the words to let her know what was happening.

"There's a patrol car outside," he said, his eyes locked on Ross and the gun.

TWENTY

J ENNIFER pushed herself away from the table, stunned by Ross's fury. He was standing in the middle of the room, screaming like a maniac.

He shot a wild-eyed look of fury at Jennifer. "A patrol car just came down the hill! Two cops and her old man!"

Hugging her arms to her chest, Jennifer backed as far away from Ross as she could get. She prayed frantically that the fact that the police car was coming *down* the hill meant that they had already checked Thomas Power's place and were about to stop here in search of Whitney.

Without taking his eyes off Ross, who had turned to watch the door, Michael silently mouthed the words to Whitney.

"Two policemen—and Daniel."

A look of hope flared high in her eyes and held.

Jennifer moved alongside Whitney's chair and gave her shoulder a quick squeeze.

Ross whipped around. *"You—"* He screamed an oath at Jennifer, then bolted across the room to the window. His back to the wall, he peered out of the dusty glass, watching.

As if he only then remembered that Jennifer was still unbound, he waved the gun at her. "Get on that chair—where you were before! I don't want you to move. I don't want you to *breathe!"* When Jennifer hesitated, he roared at her. *"Do it!"*

Jennifer vaulted to the chair, turning just enough that she could still watch Ross out of the corner of her eye.

He began to babble, making no sense. A tremor of dread shook Jennifer. What if Ross completely lost it, went out of control? What would happen to them?

"Didn't even get the Bronco out of sight," he muttered. "This is going to spoil everything. . . . We'll have to leave . . . go somewhere else . . . start all over again. . . ."

Jennifer looked at Michael across from her. His features were rigid, his gaze fixed on Ross.

Everyone but Whitney jumped when a voice suddenly came over the patrol car's loudspeaker.

"Ross, this is the police! Come out before anyone gets hurt. We've got you surrounded—throw down your weapon and come out hands up!"

Jennifer cried out as Ross shattered the windowpane with his gun. "Listen up! I've got three people in here—two women and a cop—and not one of them is coming out alive unless I walk. You got that?"

There was silence for a moment, then another voice cut in. *"Ross—this is Daniel Kaine."*

Jennifer's hand went to her mouth as she choked off a sob.

"You've got my wife in there. Listen to me. I'm blind, and I'm on crutches. I'm no threat to you. Send the women out, and let me come in."

"No!" Jennifer gasped, shooting up off her chair. "Daniel—"

Without turning, Ross yelled at her. "Shut up! And get back where you belong!"

For a moment there was silence in the cabin and on the road. Then the sound of tires squealed as another car came roaring up the road.

"State police!" Ross choked out. He whipped around, and Jennifer caught her breath at his face. Sweat had splotched the white makeup. The black paint around his eyes was smeared. His mouth was a red gash, open and panting.

Jennifer's blood chilled as she stared at him. He looked almost inhuman. And thoroughly evil.

Unexpectedly, he veered away from the window and charged across the room, waving the gun in their direction as he backed up to the open doorway that led into the other room.

"Don't move," he warned them.

The three of them watched as he yanked something off the bed and tossed it at Michael. Hurriedly, he hoisted the gun under his arm and untied the detective.

"Stay put; don't even blink," he muttered, yanking the rope away with shaky hands.

As soon as the rope dropped away from Michael's wrists, Ross straightened and aimed the gun at Whitney's head.

"Put that on," he told the detective, motioning to the black-and-white Pierrot costume he had thrown at him. "Just pull it over your clothes—hurry up, get it on! Try anything, and I blow her out the window!"

Michael moved, grimacing at the pain when he hauled himself out of the chair. Without a word, he pulled the ballooning clown pants over his jeans, yanked the tunic over his head, then pulled the skullcap down over his hair.

Jennifer marveled at the outward calm of the detective.

"Do your face," Ross ordered shortly, motioning to the makeup kit. "Like mine. Fast!"

Michael hesitated, glancing from Ross to the makeup. Ross pushed the gun against the back of Whitney's head. *Do it, cop!* he shouted.

Jennifer could feel Michael's rage as he smeared the clown white over his face with an incredibly steady hand, then swabbed the red greasepaint around his mouth, finally rimming his eyes with black.

She glanced at Whitney. The look in her eyes and the tears spilling down her painted cheeks told Jennifer everything. Whitney loved this man.

"All right," Devlin said matter-of-factly. "How's this?"

Ross seemed to quiet a little as he appraised the other man's appearance. Then he nodded. "Not bad for an amateur."

Jennifer listened with incredulity to this mundane exchange between the two.

Ross went back to the shattered window. "OK, cops. You give me free passage, I'll bring everyone out. Otherwise, they're all dead. I'll shoot them first, then myself. What's it going to be?"

After a long silence, a voice Jennifer recognized as Rick Hill's came over the loudspeaker. *"What do you want, Ross?"*

"I go to the Bronco—nobody moves until I get inside and drive down the hill." He waited, breathing heavily, eyeing the three at the table as he pointed the gun at them.

Silence. Then, *"All right, you've got it. Send the two women out first, and nobody touches you."*

Ross hesitated, then moved to free Whitney, pulling her up from the chair and holding her captive with an arm locked around her neck.

He pointed the gun at Jennifer. "Go."

Blinking back tears, Jennifer looked at Whitney, then turned and went out the door. Her legs were shaking so violently she prayed she'd make it off the porch without falling. She ran toward the police cars, only vaguely aware of the buzzing activity taking place between the two city policemen and the state police. She saw only Daniel, propped on his crutch, leaning against the side of the cruiser. His face was haggard, his expression stricken.

As soon as she cried out his name, he pushed himself away from the car and began to limp toward her. From inside the patrol car, Sunny began to bark fiercely, but Daniel didn't seem to hear. Reaching him, Jennifer threw her arms around his waist. For a moment, she could do nothing but sob helplessly against him.

Finally, she turned to Rick Hill. "Ross doesn't have any intention of letting Whitney go!" she told the policeman. "He's going to take her with him if you let him get away! And he'll *kill* Michael Devlin—he's a police detective!"

"We know, Mrs. Kaine." The officer's quiet, level voice steadied her. "What about weapons? What has Ross got?"

"Two guns. Ross has on a clown suit!" Jennifer choked out. "And he made Michael put on one just like it. You won't be able to tell them apart when they—"

The words died in her throat as she saw the police officer's gaze go to the cabin. With her arms still locked around Daniel, Jennifer turned to look.

On the porch were Michael and Ross, both in black-and-white Pierrot costumes, with Whitney between them.

One of the state policemen muttered a groan of frustration as the trio came down the steps and started toward the road. "Which one is *which?* We can't risk shooting."

They were halfway to the cars when without warning one of the Pierrots let go of Whitney, shoving her out and away from them. *"Run, Whitney!"* he shouted at her, at the same time whirling around to throw himself at the other clown.

With his gun drawn, Rick Hill ran to pull Whitney to safety. One of the state policemen immediately joined them, pushing Whitney behind him and blocking her with his body.

One of the Pierrots pulled a gun from beneath his tunic. The other high-kicked it, sending it flying into the brush several feet away. At that, his opponent bolted across the road, running uphill in the direction of the parked Bronco. The other followed in fierce pursuit.

Rick Hill turned to Whitney, touching her shoulder to get her attention.

"Can you tell them apart, Miss Sharyn? Do you know which man is Detective Tierney?"

Jennifer looked at him in surprise. "You know his real name?"

"Yes, ma'am. We've known since he first arrived in town. We've been working together on this."

Whitney clutched his arm. "I can't tell, not from here. Take me closer. I need to be sure."

The state policeman in front of her turned. "No, ma'am. It wouldn't be safe."

Leaving Whitney with one officer, the two city patrolmen and the other state trooper began to move up the road, weapons leveled at the two Pierrots now wrestling near the Bronco.

Jennifer felt Whitney move and cried out. But Whitney was already flying across the road and running up the hill toward the Pierrots.

Jennifer started after her, but the state policeman put a restraining hand on her arm. "I'll get her. Stay here with your husband." Immediately, he took off across the road, his gun in hand as he raced up the hill behind Whitney.

Jennifer clung to Daniel, watching. Suddenly another gun appeared. "One of them has the other gun!" she cried out. "I can't tell if it's Michael or Ross!" Daniel's arm tightened around her shoulder.

"Oh, no—Whitney's going right to them!"

Daniel held her as she tried to wrest free. "You can't *do* anything, Jennifer! You'll just make it harder for the police."

Both Pierrots were now on their feet, dangerously close to the edge of the cliff as they struggled for the gun.

Horrified, Jennifer saw Whitney suddenly turn and head directly for the rim of the drop-off, stopping no more than a foot away from the edge.

She hesitated, turned to the police, then back to the struggling clowns. *"Michael,* help me! Help me!"

She moved right to the edge of the cliff, weaving as she looked down.

The clowns turned, one with a gun in the air, the other in a crouch as he struggled to keep his footing. Two stunned, bewildered white faces gaped at Whitney. Then one bolted and started to run, crying her name as she plunged over the edge.

The Pierrot with the gun aimed at the running man and fired. The wounded Pierrot grabbed his shoulder but didn't stop. He glanced down when he reached the rim of the drop-off, then straightened and jumped over.

Jennifer screamed and broke free of Daniel's arms. He tried to call her back, but she went on, reaching the road just as another shot rang out. She looked up the hill in time to see the other Pierrot fall to the ground.

She reached the edge of the cliff and dropped to her knees, still sobbing. She caught her breath as she stared down at the scene below her in stunned disbelief. There, in the middle of a wide, shelflike extension, stood the injured Pierrot—Michael—holding Whitney in his arms!

Jennifer watched them for a moment, started to call out, then stopped. Finally, assured that they were safe, she drew back to give them some privacy.

Michael's gruff, unsteady voice reached Jennifer's ears as she started to turn away. "That was a daft thing to do! You could have been killed! Whatever made you try such an idiotic stunt?"

"I had to make sure the police wouldn't shoot the wrong man."

At his muffled exclamation, Whitney went on. "I had to get you away from Cory, to . . . separate you . . . so the police would have a chance at him. I had to do *something.*" She paused. "I thought you would remember about the shelf . . . that it would break my fall."

"I *forgot* about the shelf! I forgot *everything* when I saw you going over that cliff!"

"But you jumped anyway," Whitney replied after a moment.

"You meant it, didn't you, Michael, when you told me that if I ever needed you . . . you'd come to me."

He missed only a beat. "Of course, I meant it. But how could you be so certain that all those other policemen out there would would recognize me?"

There was a brief pause. "Why, Michael Devlin Tierney, I should think you, of all people, should trust a fellow officer to know the good guys from the bad."

Silence descended, and Jennifer moved to hold off the approaching policemen for at least another moment.

Shepherd Valley, West Virginia
Christmas Eve

FROM her vantage point in the choir loft, Jennifer looked out over the crowded sanctuary, aglow with candles and decked with holly and evergreens. Her heart warmed as her gaze came to rest on Jason, nestled between his grandparents. He grinned at her and waved the small candle he would be lighting later in the service.

Gabe and Lyss were both in the choir loft, of course—Lyss beside her, and Gabe at the end of the row. Jennifer glanced over at the organ where Daniel, finally free of his cast, had begun to play quiet carols in preparation for the Christmas Eve worship service.

A stirring at the back of the shadowed sanctuary caught Jennifer's attention. As she watched, Thomas Power, leaning on his walker, made his way to the front. Jennifer wondered if the aging miner had ever set foot inside a church before tonight. But here he was, with Whitney at his elbow and Michael Devlin—Michael Devlin *Tierney*, she corrected herself—right behind them. Thomas Power appeared less formidable in the candlelight, Jennifer observed. She actually thought she detected the ghost of a smile when, near the front of the sanctuary, Whitney and Michael helped the elderly gentleman into a pew right behind Daniel's parents.

It seemed that Whitney's gentle persistence had wrought a

change in the lonely old man. Not to mention the change she had wrought in the handsome Irish policeman at her side, Jennifer thought. Whitney glanced up in her direction just then, and they exchanged a smile. Michael, seated beside her, was in uniform tonight in his capacity as a brand-new addition to the Shepherd Valley police force. He, too, was wearing a huge smile. Probably, Jennifer thought with no small feeling of satisfaction, because he and Whitney were to be married on New Year's Eve.

They were a handsome couple, no doubt about it. Michael, of course, had redeemed himself in Jennifer's eyes by stating his intention to settle down in Shepherd Valley . . . with Whitney. And Whitney, finally safe from Cory Ross, who had died by his own hand that awful day on the mountain, fairly floated through life these days, secure with her newly gained freedom and unmistakable happiness.

As for her husband-to-be, Michael, in his own words, had "come home." He had returned to the God of his childhood, returned to the faith he had once thought lost to him forever. He had also joined Whitney by involving himself in the life of the community, bringing to it the same fierce energy and commitment he seemed to apply to everything else he did.

Jennifer didn't realize that her long sigh of contentment had been audible until Lyss elbowed her. She straightened a little then and continued to scan the sanctuary, cherishing it all: the candlelight, the music, the families joined together, and the love that seemed to permeate their midst.

Near the end of the service, after all the candles had been lighted and most of the beloved, familiar carols sung, Daniel, with the help of a cane, came to lead the choir in a hushed, a cappella arrangement of "O Come, O Come, Emmanuel." At the same time, Whitney rose and made her way to the platform, stepping to one side of the choir loft, where she could see both the choir and the congregation.

As the choir rose and began to sing, Whitney began to sign, gracefully, fervently, the words to the old hymn. Her hands seemed to soar in a harmony all their own. Her face was radiant with joy, as if her entire being was absorbed with the miraculous, transforming truth the words of the hymn communicated. . . .

"O come, O come, Emmanuel . . . and ransom captive Israel. . . ."

Jennifer's eyes misted. *Emmanuel . . . God with us . . .* The Christ, the Son of God, had come to set the captives free, to bring the freedom only he could give. Freedom for Whitney Sharyn, from her prison of fear and the torment of a madman's obsession. For Michael Devlin Tierney, from his self-imposed isolation. For Thomas Power, from years of loneliness and regret. Freedom for all who would open their hearts and accept it.

At the end, Daniel turned to face the congregation, who joined hands with one another as he began to pray. . . .

"Dear Lord and Father . . . may we join hearts as well as hands tonight. Bring us together as we have never been before, and help us to realize how greatly we are blessed to be standing here with those we love on yet another Christmas Eve. Let us be aware that we may never be together in quite this way again, for with the passing of each year, life brings change. Tonight is a gift—a gift to be held gently, with great care, a gift to be treasured.

"Before we leave this place tonight, Father, to go home to the trees and the gifts, to share the dreams and the memories that are such a precious part of this holy season, let us look at one another with our hearts and really *see* each other: our husbands and our wives, our parents and our children, our sweethearts, our neighbors, and our friends. Let us take the time to say, 'I love you. . . . you're a gift from God to me.'

"For that's the true gift of Christmas, Father . . . your love for us and ours for one another. We thank you for this incredible, priceless gift of love. And this Christmas, we pray that you will teach us to *be* a people of love. Teach us to love you . . . to love one another . . . while we can.

"Amen."

Collect all the titles in the Daybreak Mysteries series by B. J. Hoff